Moonshine
and
Watermelons

AND OTHER OZARK TALES

MARK VAN PATTEN

PAGE PUBLISHING, INC.
Conneaut Lake, PA

First originally published by Page Publishing 2020

ISBN 978-1-6624-0376-7 (pbk)
ISBN 978-1-6624-0377-4 (digital)

Printed in the United States of America

I dedicate this book to the memory of my granny and gramps, George and Mildred Van Patten. Their sacrifices to raise me have earned them sainthood.

CONTENTS

FOREWORD

The stories you're about to enjoy were lived, and written, by a very special guy. Okay, so he's embellished the truth a little every now and then, but only he knows where, when, and how much, and that's just fine by me.

I've fished with Mark and shared a friend's peppermint candy-flavored moonshine with him. Maybe I'll get to share a purloined watermelon with him someday too. It's on my "to-do" list for sure.

As he tells it, Mark left home and west-coast gangland at a tender age and hitchhiked halfway across an unfamiliar continent to begin life anew with his granny and gramps in the Ozark hills. And, my, what a life it turned out to be!

If you were ever young yourself, I'm sure you'll chuckle yourself silly over Mark's telling of his youthful adventures and misadventures. Perhaps you'll even be reminded of your own younger years. I hope so. Such delightful and heartwarming shenanigans aren't confined only to young boys or the Ozarks.

I also hope I can convince Mark to pen a sequel to these fascinating pages someday. Surely, he hasn't revealed all of the youthful mischief he got into so many years ago, or even more recently.

Carry on, folks. You're gonna love it!

—*Chuck Tryon*

ACKNOWLEDGMENTS

I want to acknowledge all the wonderful people who shared their lives with me as I grew up in the Ozarks. Most importantly, I want to acknowledge the one who always believes in me, my best half, my life mate, and the best darn cook since my granny, my wife, Regina.

I couldn't have had these adventures to share if it hadn't been for my best friend. He was, still is, and always will be Donald Ray. I want to thank Joel Vance for his persistence in helping me realize the importance of recording these events before the memories faded beyond recollection. I cannot forget Spencer Turner, the "Rotund Biologist" who inspired me to write my first article many years ago. I also want to thank my old friend, fellow author and mentor, Chuck Tryon, who pushed and urged me to submit this manuscript to a publisher. I would like to thank Mary Utrecht, a fellow aspiring author, who helped motivate me, and without whose grammatical guidance, no publisher would have taken a second glance at this manuscript.

PRELUDE

The Ozarks conveys a different mental image for everyone. Some visualize long black beards, moonshine whiskey, and corncob pipes, while others imagine canoe trips down clear, free-flowing, gravel-bottom streams, oak, and hickory forests, a log cabin nestled in a wooded grove, and a wisp of blue-gray smoke floating above a native stone chimney.

I lived a spell in the Ozarks. Life was hard and taken seriously. At the same time, the folks who scratched out a living from the rocky ground never lost their sense of humor. The harder life is, the more humor is needed to carry on with the daily challenges.

I've taken certain journalistic liberties with many of the events I have recorded here. The people are real. The personalities are as I remember them. Some of the events may be exaggerated. Actually, "may be" is a little weak. They are either as I remember them or as I would like to remember them.

I have changed some names not so much to protect the innocent, but to protect the privacy that country folk hold so dear. Any outsider who has ever visited Ozark folk can tell you—they are a private lot. They don't cotton to talk about others by anyone, and they don't tolerate talk about themselves or their family.

Changing the names is for my protection as well. I would hate to lose fishing rights to some of my favorite spots. Oh, and by the way, any resemblance in name or personality to individuals alive or

deceased not wanting to be included in this book is purely coinciden-
tal. I didn't want you in here either.

It is my hope this book will allow you to meet and appreciate
some of the most wonderful characters and personalities that life has
to offer.

I am at the age when remembering those youthful summer
afternoons and cold-as-a-well-digger's-rear-end winter mornings in
the Ozarks is getting harder to recall. Honestly, I wrote this book so
I could relive my youth by remembering the way homemade *moonshine* can suck the breath out of your lungs and savoring the sweet
juice of a *watermelon* stolen from old Rube's melon patch as it drib-
bled down my chin on a hot August afternoon.

CHAPTER 1

Chewed-Up Turtles

At the grand age of twelve, I left my home, my mother, two younger sisters, and my little brother to escape some of the problems I faced growing up in a rough part of the San Francisco Bay Area. Gangs, drugs, and peer pressure had drawn me into a world of death and fear. At a very young age, I had been forced to fight to survive. I wanted out and knew the only option was to go far away for a while.

I remembered I had grandparents living in a place called Missouri. I heard they lived on a small, working cattle ranch, and I was excited at the prospect of farm life, even if just for a laugh. But first, I had to find them.

Under the watchful eye of a very busy and seriously stressed-out guardian angel, an over-the-road truck driver, and an old farmer by the name of Red Mulligan in a beat-up 1952 Chevy pickup, I found my way to the front porch of the Lazy G, my grandparent's farm. The G was for George, my grandfather.

My big-city ignorance of country life could only imagine scenes from "Old McDonald's farm." What did I know about chiggers, ticks, and cow piles? All would be revealed to me as a young boy in a new world filled with adventures I could never have imagined back in the city.

I peered into the darkness as Red's pickup truck slowed and made a sharp turn into the gravel drive at the home of my grandparents. I opened the door, climbed out, and stretched to squeeze out some of the stiffness in my young legs. I looked up and was momentarily mesmerized by the ink-black sky lit up like a Christmas tree. I was taken by surprise at how many stars Missouri had. Light pollution back in the city never allowed the stars to show with such brilliance.

The night was black dark. The light cast from the stars did nothing to reveal my surroundings. There was no moon, and I felt a bit claustrophobic, trying to peer through the darkness. Being a city boy, I was used to the lights of the city. I had never experienced that kind of darkness. It felt like a wall surrounding me, closing in on all sides with no escape possible. A young boy's fear of the dark swelled in my throat. I squeaked a barely audible "Thanks" to Red as he rounded the circle and clattered his way down the drive back to the two-lane blacktop road known as "U" highway.

Just as a Boogeyman paranoia started to take over my senses, a rectangular glow appeared and seemed to float for a second in the darkness as a door opened. A light flashed on, revealing a concrete porch with four steps leading up to the door.

Movement in the amber glow of the porch light caught my eye. A man stood in the doorway. He was pushing back a cat with his toe. The cat obviously wanted in the house badly.

The man's body blocked much of the light coming through the door. His silhouette revealed a short, stocky frame and a close-cut flattop haircut that shined of platinum gray in the light from the interior of the house. Impatiently he waved to me after losing the battle with the cat.

I had everything I owned packed in a small suitcase. Red had retrieved it from the back of the truck and set it on the ground before leaving. I picked it up and prepared to meet my grandparents. I slowly walked toward the man on the front porch. He squinted to see who I was and turned to speak to someone inside the house.

"It looks like Sparkie," he said with hope and reservation in his voice.

Sparkie was the nickname they had given to my dad when he was a young boy. He had left my mother and us kids when I was six years old and gone to Mexico to escape repercussions for the life he had chosen. He had broken the hearts of all who loved him and left, never to return until they day he came home in a casket in the spring of my sixteenth year. I was unaware of the meaning of the nickname and spoke for the first time.

"No, it's not Sparkie. My name is Mark. I think I am your grandson."

My grandmother burst through the door, nearly knocking my grandfather off the porch. She stood in the porch light, drying her hands on an apron tied around her waist. My grandfather stood five feet, nine inches tall, dwarfing my grandmother as she closed in on four feet, eight inches. Her short physical stature was not a deterrent from anything my grandmother set her mind to. I would learn this lesson many times over in the years to come. In spite of the fact that I would exceed six feet later on, I would always look up to these two people with respect and love. My grandmother's pearl-gray hair was a beacon that drew me home on the darkest of nights, knowing she would be there to provide me with love and always a full belly.

"Sparkie's boy?" she asked tentatively.

I didn't know if I was Sparkie's boy.

"I don't know. I live in California with my mom, my sister Joyce, my brother Randall, and my baby sister Loretta."

That old lady jumped from the porch without hitting any of the steps and had her plump arms around me, crying and laughing while suffocating me in her ample bosom at the same time before I could drop my suitcase. She kissed my face and hugged me harder than I had ever been hugged. I could smell the enticing aroma of something cooking; a generic aroma that represented spice and all the familiar foods a young boy loves as she was hugging me. My stomach started to growl. My grandfather, still standing on the porch, was trying to coax us into the house. I glanced around at my surroundings as I was headed toward the porch.

It was difficult to tell much about the outside of the house in the obscurity of the night. It appeared to be a small white farmhouse with a big front yard. What was behind the house? There was no way to know with that wall of black standing solidly just at the edge of the porch-light glow. It was mid-November. A chill in the night air pressed in as we climbed the porch steps. A wall of warm air met us as we walked through the door.

I smelled burning wood. What was on fire? My grandfather was bent over, putting a piece of a tree in a huge brown box-looking thing with a pipe coming out the back and going up to the ceiling. I could see the orange glow of fire and sparks shooting out through the open door of a woodburning stove. I had never seen a woodburning stove in my long twelve years of life. *That's neat,* I thought. Fire always intrigues a young boy.

Handshakes and hugs of welcome were plentiful. My grandmother insisted that I eat something. We could talk about how and why I had arrived here in the morning. Eating first, I would learn later, was the normal drill. A black-and-white television, tuned to one of the two channels they were able to receive, caught my eye. These folks weren't that backward. They had TV.

My grandfather picked up my suitcase and carried it off somewhere. My grandmother told me to relax on the couch in the living room while she "fixed a bite to eat." I stretched out on the overstuffed couch and watched some guy named Slim Wilson singing a country song. The warmth of the woodstove and weariness from my travels took its toll. My eyelids got heavier and heavier.

My grandparents were the epitome of the expression, "The salt of the earth." They were just good, plain folk that cared about their neighbors as much as they did about their family. They lived by the golden rule and expected everyone else did as well. It would never occur to them to do otherwise. They both had survived the depression and were not prone to throw away much that had any use at all.

My grandfather's family had homesteaded in Colorado in the mid-1800s. "The fever" ravaged neighboring farms and finally hit home for my grandfather's family. His mother and older brother were gravely ill.

At the suggestion of a local doctor who had migrated from Swedeborg, Missouri, my grandfather's dad, Levi, sold his farm, bought a covered wagon, and headed east to Missouri. Along the way, my grandfather's sixteen-year-old brother died. They buried him beside the wagon trail somewhere in Kansas. The family settled on a farm near Clinton, Missouri. Cora, my grandfather's mother, survived the fever. Levi and Cora started from scratch, trying to make a life for the remaining family, raising row crops on a river-bottom farm.

At the age of nineteen, my grandfather took his first real paying job as a railroad-depot agent in Steelville, Missouri. That was where he met and married my grandmother. After leaving Kentucky in search of better farming land, my grandmother's family settled along the Meramec River in the area now known as the Woodson K Woods Conservation Area. My grandmother had six sisters and one brother. The brother was the youngest. After seven girls, they finally got a son to help out on the farm and decided eight mouths were enough to feed.

To help out with the finances, the oldest daughter—my grandmother—went into Steelville to get a job. She landed her first job waiting tables in a popular café where it just so happened my single and suave grandfather ate nearly every day. After courting for a year, they were married. About two years later my lineage began.

My grandfather had one major vice. His vice was shared by my grandmother. They both loved to fish. He liked to fly fish and, in time, had converted my grandmother from bait chucking to fly-fishing. He was always on the prowl for a new stream to fish and had a propensity for finding spring-fed creeks along the railroad. When the demand for trout in fancy restaurants back east compelled entrepreneurs to build fish hatcheries in Chicago and New York, carloads of trout fingerlings were shipped cross-country from northern California in old-style milk cans with holes drilled in the lids. They had to be shipped in the winter to keep the water cold enough for the fingerling trout to survive.

My grandfather convinced his buddies that rode the railroad cars to "accidentally" drop a milk-can load of fingerlings in spring creeks the train would cross over or run alongside. That was how some of the wild populations of trout on their way to a fish hatchery found permanent homes in Missouri streams.

When my dad was knee-high to a grasshopper, my grandfather was offered a job working for a major oil company at a pipeline pumping station near Kneebone, Missouri. He bought forty acres that joined the pump-station land for $200. He also purchased one of the houses that the company had provided to its employees for $50 and had it moved onto his newly acquired land. The year was 1933. An adjoining 40-acre parcel was purchased the next year for $200.00. That piece of the farm was of course called the "back forty." Doesn't every farm have a back forty? The Lazy G would be home for three generations.

"Soup's on!"

My eyes popped open in surprise. Where was I? The smell of something delicious coming from the direction of the small dining room gave rise to a mental comment: *Who cares? I smell food.*

I jumped up from the cozy, old couch and headed straight to the source of the aroma that had set in motion a grumbling stomach and a watering mouth.

There on the table was the biggest spread of food I had ever witnessed. There was fried chicken, mashed potatoes and chicken gravy, peas, corn on the cob, homemade biscuits, a tall glass of cold milk, and a piece of pie that had a purple berry-looking stuff oozing out from under the perfectly browned, flakey crust. A scoop of vanilla ice cream slid down the side of the fresh-baked pie as it melted from the still-warm-from-the-oven piece of heaven.

My grandmother's voice snapped me back to earth, "I threw together a few leftovers since it was so late. I hope you don't mind."

Mind? Was she nuts? Let's eat! I was about to discover that my grandmother was internationally known, at least in this county, as the best darn cook ever.

When I finally pushed away from the table, there was little left to consume. The plate and serving bowls were void of the once-magnificent feast. A dribble here and a spot of crust there was all that remained.

My grandfather had mentioned a few chores I was to take on, which I only heard part of during my eating binge. One of the things I recalled Gramps mentioning was feeding the dogs. That was okay by me. I loved dogs. I wasn't sure what "getting the wood in" meant, but if it had anything to do with making a fire in the stove, that was okay too.

For lack of a better idea, I had started calling my grandparents "Granny" and "Gramps." It was shorter and easier than Grandmother and Grandfather. Besides, they didn't really come across as formal types to me. They seemed fine with that, so it stuck.

After Granny had cleared the table and washed the dishes, she told me to grab a coat and help her feed the dogs. Since this was to be my job, I decided that I would follow along. By this time, I was nursing an uncomfortable, overstuffed feeling in my stomach. Granny had on a worn, red plaid flannel coat with the sleeves frayed at the wrists. She carried a small white bucket in one hand and a flashlight in the other. We went out the front-porch door and headed around toward the back of the house. It was absolutely pitch-black.

Granny opened a small metal gate and headed across what I assumed was the backyard. I could hear the dogs jumping and whining for their supper, so I knew we were close to their pen. As Granny swept the flashlight back and forth, something unusual caught my eye.

"Wait a minute, Granny, what was that?"

"What was what?"

"That," I said as I pointed into the dark at something on the ground.

She handed me the flashlight and asked me to show her what I was talking about. I grabbed the light and searched the ground until I found it.

I stared at the object on the ground and exclaimed, "Look, Granny, the dogs chewed up a turtle."

Granny glanced at the dark blob spotlighted by the flashlight and laughed so hard she nearly dropped the dog's food bucket.

"Child, that's not a chewed-up turtle. It's a cow pile the chickens picked at."

I was not only embarrassed for not knowing that, I was irritated at the fact that I still didn't know what she was talking about.

Humbly, I said, "Oh, what kind of dogs are these?" trying to move Granny's attention to something else.

That was the first of many experiences this city boy would not be allowed to forget.

CHAPTER 2

Hillbilly Twilight Zone

Sunday night, Granny said I needed to get to bed early. Then she dropped the bombshell.

"You'll be starting school in the morning."

What? Did she say school? I thought I was on sabbatical. I didn't know it included school. I crawled into bed and started to think about school.

I imagined a one-room log cabin and a mean-looking woman whacking poor, unsuspecting kids over the head with a yardstick for wrong answers. I trembled at the thought. It wasn't long before the visions dancing around behind my eyelids began to fade. The triple layer of Granny's hand-quilted blankets and a goose-down feather-tick mattress was too much for my wild and nervous imagination. I dreamed of many things.

I had watched enough cartoons to recognize the crow of a rooster when I heard one. I heard one. I sat up in bed like a spring-loaded mouse trap. There it was again. I looked outside and saw some chickens picking around an old white building badly in need of a paint job (the building, not the chickens). I had arrived at the farm late the night before and had no idea what was behind the house except for dogs and cow piles (whatever they were). I heard someone putting wood in the wood stove. The door opened, and there stood

Granny, wiping her hands on an apron. The smell of bacon frying blew through the door from behind her like a gust of wind. This was going to be a great day! I was smiling from ear to ear. I love bacon!

Granny smiled back and said, "Better hurry. We have to get to school early enough to get you registered before the first bell." The look on my face must have been obvious.

"Every boy your age needs an education. Clothes are washed, mended, ironed, and on the back of the chair there. Say, are those the only clothes you brought?"

I had brought an extra pair of jeans with the knees out, a T-shirt with a black-and-white picture of the Golden Gate Bridge on it, a pair of socks, and one pair of underwear.

"Breakfast will be ready in ten minutes. Don't be late, or the dogs will get yours," she said with a grin.

School! My shoulders suddenly felt heavy as I trudged to the bathroom. The bathroom was really different from what I was used to. First of all, it had no heat and was cold. Man, when you sat down on that white throne, you had better take care of business quickly, or someone might be calling the fire department to defrost your backside from it. I had heard stories about people's skin freezing to cold stuff.

The wallpaper reminded me of something right out of an old Western movie. It was a combination of red velvet and gold shiny tinsel with a paisley print. The windows had so many coats of white paint they were stuck shut. The ceiling, which had last been wallpapered in 1930, was sagging from years of humidity from hot showers in a cold room. Once the mirror on the wall fogged up, you could forget using it to comb your hair. Yep, things were different out here in the country. But at least they had indoor plumbing.

After a breakfast consisting of eggs, bacon, biscuits and gravy, homemade bread toasted and slathered with molasses and butter, Granny and I headed for school. The drive to the little town where the school stood was fascinating. I saw cows standing around in large fields of dried brown grass and dark-gray wooded forests devoid of leaves. This was a new experience for me. We didn't have seasons in the part of California that I was from.

I half expected to see a real town when we drove into the little village of Pine Ridge on the banks of the roaring Roubidoux Creek. There was a gas station, a post office, a bank, and a general store. A few old houses lined the ancient, pot-holed streets. To my total surprise, there was not a log cabin, but a group of modern buildings where the school stood.

Yellow school busses were just arriving, and I saw kids of every age. More importantly, I saw kids my age. Granny led me to the superintendent's office to register me for school. I never saw a school where kids from kindergarten to high school were in the same place. We had different schools for elementary, junior high, and high school back home. The school was small compared to the one I attended in California, but it looked pretty normal for a school until I was shown to my first classroom. The principal led my Granny and me down a long hallway to the last classroom on the left. He went inside to talk to the teacher while we waited in the hall. The first kid I laid eyes on was sitting at his desk in bib overalls. *Holy cow!*

I swore I heard Rod Serling's voice whispering, *"You have just entered the hillbilly twilight zone."*

By Christmas that year, I had made it through the awkwardness of being the new kid and started making a few friends. My best friend was Donald Ray. Ray was his middle name. He and I are now late in years, and I still call him Donald Ray. I guess it was like Jim Bob or Billy Ray what's-his-name, the country singer. It's just one of those down-home familiarities we got used to using.

CHAPTER 3

The Church in the Barnyard

The first time I met Donald Ray was in church. I will never forget my first trip to the little country church I would attend most of my young life. Granny rousted me out of bed early Sunday morning. Gramps asked me if I would help him feed the cows before church. I was pretty excited about seeing the big black animals up close. I didn't realize that it would mean getting up in the dark. I grumbled at the light, spearing my sleep-heavy eyes when Granny opened the door to wake me.

"You have to get up now if you're going to get the cows fed in time for church."

"Can't we feed them after church?" I asked.

"Sure, if you don't mind waiting for your breakfast until after church as well," Granny said with a serious look on her face.

My stomach said, *"No way!"* So off to the cold bathroom I trudged.

Granny had the car all warmed up when I finished changing after helping Gramps feed the cows. I knew what a cow pile was now! I climbed into the front seat of the old Chevy with Granny, and we headed for church. We turned onto a gravel road, and I started to get a little nervous. You see, I had never been on a real gravel road before moving to the country. This was a genuine rock-strewn, washboard, dust-making gravel road. Gravel would slam into the underside of the car, making me jump. It sounded like someone was throwing rocks at us from the woods. Granny acted like she didn't notice; she was good about not embarrassing me unnecessarily. She turned the car onto a narrower gravel road and drove over what looked like a bunch of two-by-four boards standing on edge. I later learned that was a cattle guard. Cows would not walk over it, thus eliminating the need for a gate.

In a mile or so, we came to a gate across the road. Granny stopped the car and told me to get out and open it. After fumbling around with an ingenious-looking wooden lever on a wire, I managed to open the gate, which proceeded to collapse at my feet. I thought I had broken it. Granny leaned out the window and told me to stretch it tight and walk it out of the way. I figured out the gate was just some barbed wire stretched to a post by that latch thing I was messing with. After the car drove through the opening, I closed the gate.

I was trying to figure out the latch when another car pulled up to the gate. Granny waved me to the car, telling me to open the gate for them and they would latch it after they drove through. To my astonishment, it suddenly dawned on me we were driving through someone's barnyard.

I'm not kidding! There was the barn, the chickens, the cows in the middle of the road, and everything else you saw in front of a barn in a barnyard. After driving through another gate, we were traveling along a field. There weren't any fences to keep the cows out of the road, and I saw a lot of those cow-pile things in the road. Granny was a master at hitting every one of them.

The pasture faded into full woods as we drove around one exceptionally sharp bend in the road. There in front of us was a small white building with a sign that identified it as a church. We pulled into a tiny, grassy area acting as the parking lot. I noticed a small, well-kept graveyard off to the left and a tiny building that looked like it was for storing rakes or brooms or something. The building was only four feet by four feet, with a roof high enough for a grown man to stand in. A sign on it said "Women." That was very strange.

When I got out of the car and started following Granny to the front door, I noticed another one of those tiny buildings with a sign that said "Men."

My mind began to put it all together in horror. Those buildings were made of boards that looked to be over a hundred years old. The doors hung kind of lopsided, and you could see daylight through the cracks between the boards. I knew they had to be restrooms. I later learned the proper name for them was "outhouse." It was a good thing I hadn't drank my usual two glasses of orange juice and half a gallon of milk for breakfast because I wasn't about to go out to that scary-looking building. The day did come when I had to use it. That experience was a story in itself. The main character of that particular story was a big, mean, red wasp with a nasty attitude toward soft city boys.

When I first entered the church house, I knew it was old by the smell. It had a not-unpleasant aroma of old wood with a slight dusting of mold or mildew. It was erected in 1910 and was only heated on Sundays and special-event days. Decades of cold, damp air had given the church its characteristic nuance.

The front door led into what the congregation called the "anteroom." I wasn't sure what that meant. It was a narrow vestibule with a row of four seats on either side of a carpeted path leading into the church.

I had seen churches in California and knew all about the big stained-glass windows, the huge choirs with satin robes, and the comfortable padded pews. This was a far cry from what I imagined when Granny told me we were going to church. The room wasn't very well lit. The pews were old wooden theater-type seats with no padding at all. Each seat in a row was attached to the next, and the entire row was bolted down to the floor. The windows were stained, all right. There was a splash of white paint from the last time the church was painted on a number of the divided panes. An old upright piano in the front of the church sat off to the right of the pulpit. A tall, narrow, handmade pulpit stood towering in the center of a raised floor. I later learned that Donald Ray's grandfather had made the pulpit. The raised floor acted as a stage for Christmas programs, choir, and the preacher. A row of four seats like the pews lined the wall on either side of the preacher for the choir.

Granny gently nudged me ahead of her to her favorite seat. Before I sat down, I noticed a boy about my age sitting by himself in the row directly in front of where Granny was headed. Since I was new and didn't know anybody yet, and since I was never shy about making new friends, I asked Granny if I could go sit by the boy. She smiled and nodded her agreement.

Donald Ray sat slouched down in his seat with his knees up against the back of the pew in front of him. His head was down in concentration. He appeared to be reading his Bible. I sidled my way to the seat beside him and sat down. He didn't seem to notice for a minute or two.

"Are you the big-city kid that moved in with Mildred?"

"Yes. My name is Mark. What's yours?"

"Donald Ray," he said nervously, looking back down at the Bible in his lap.

Donald Ray was very shy when he was young. I broke him of that.

I sat back in the chair and tried to get comfortable. It was a difficult task to get comfortable in those old wooden seats. About halfway through the sermon, Donald Ray handed me a note. *"Want to hang out after church?"* was written on a small notebook page. Donald Ray never went anywhere without a small, pocket-size notebook in his shirt pocket. He handed me the pencil, and I scribbled my response. *"Sure, if it's okay with Granny."*

I sat through the rest of the sermon without another word or note from Donald Ray. Immediately after the closing prayer I turned around in my seat to ask Granny if it would be okay to go with Donald Ray. She said I could, and when I turned back around, he was already on his way out the door. I threaded my way toward the door with a number of polite "thank-yous" for members of the congregation who expressed their delight at seeing me in church and were welcoming me to the community. The people in that church were very friendly. But all I was interested in was finding out what adventures two boys could get into on a sunny November day.

I made my way out toward the parking area. Donald Ray was standing next to an old red pickup truck. The right fender was green, and the left fender was barely hanging on. He waved me over, jumping into the driver's seat. It never occurred to me that he would drive anywhere. After all, he was only eleven years old. As soon as I slid into the passenger side, he started the motor and took off down the road. I sat paralyzed from the brain down.

My mind was screaming questions like *"What are you doing?"* *"Where are you taking me?"* *"Am I going to die?"*

All that came out of my mouth was, "Your dad is going to kill us."

Donald Ray looked sideways at me and laughed. "Pa lets me drive on gravel roads."

That's fine, I thought. *But what about the law? We would both end up in jail. I know it, I know it, I know it!*

CHAPTER 4

Critter in the Church

The rest of that winter was a blur of school, snow, feeding cows, church, Christmas, and freezing in the bathroom. Just about the time small buds on tree limbs were swelling with the promise of warmer weather, I took my first real paying job. I was paid $7.50 per month to keep the church clean and an extra $5.00 per month to mow the graveyard in the summer. Later in May I entered the church Saturday evening as was my usual tactic. I put off the job until the last minute. I justified it by saying I was saving energy. I would turn on the heat or air conditioning the night before Sunday service instead of days before.

I grabbed the vacuum cleaner from its appointed station and rolled it to the front of the church. I smelled a strong, musky odor. It wasn't something I could just ignore. It was barking at my senses like a big dog. I had smelled it before. I just couldn't recall when, where, or what it was.

The smell went from an annoying odor to a gut-wrenching, foul smell. My eyes were watering with each labored step as I tried to vacuum the floor. In desperation for a lung full of clean air, I turned to run for the door. There, two feet in front of me, was an animal of some kind. It was all black except for a white streak down its back. I had seen one of these in cartoons. It was a skunk. That must be what that smell was.

I didn't know about skunk behavior, but I could tell it was agitated. It kept turning its tail toward me and peeing. Wait a minute. That liquid spraying at me wasn't pee. It was the source of lost opportunity, lonely days ahead, and more importantly, no church for a while. Man, I was going to get in trouble big time. I didn't know what to do.

I ran for the door and slammed it shut to keep the skunk from following me. I jumped on my bicycle and pedaled as hard as I could toward Gene Berry's house. He was the guy that owned the barnyard we had to go through to get to church. I was shouting Gene's name when I rolled up to his front porch. Gene was hard of hearing, but had no problem understanding the situation when the wind shifted in his direction. He grabbed a shotgun and jumped in his truck. I tried to catch a ride but was politely told to ride my bike.

When I got to the church, Gene was standing at the door. It was still closed. He looked at me and asked why I'd shut the door.

"Did the skunk run out?"

"No," I replied. "I locked him in so you could get him."

Gene patiently explained that if I had left the door open, the skunk would have left on his own.

Gene opened the door to the anteroom. He looked around carefully. I watched as he used all his senses, obviously tuned as an expert skunk hunter. With shotgun in hand, he eased through the door. I was right on his heels. He turned and held a finger to his lips. His eyes were watering, and he appeared to be trying to hold his breath. Heck, by now I was already getting used to the smell.

The skunk was nowhere in sight. This made Gene visibly more nervous. His eyes darted into every shadow and corner. He whispered to me to hold the door open in case the skunk tried to make a getaway.

I wasn't sure what he meant by that. I held the door open. All of a sudden, Gene came rushing toward me, waving that shotgun and yelling like a madman. I nearly wet my pants thinking he had gone mad and was going to kill me for messing up the church. You see,

Gene was a deacon in the church and was probably taking this whole skunk deal pretty seriously.

Then I saw the skunk running in front of Gene, headed for the open door. Was I supposed to hold the door open and let it out? Or was I supposed to shut the door so Gene could shoot it? Which was it?

I shut the door at the last second. The skunk slammed into the closed door and immediately caught an attitude toward Gene. It turned, held its tail high, and was about to spray. Realizing that I had trapped this wild animal in the church, Gene began to fumble with the safety on his gun. The skunk was about to spray him at point-blank range. He raised his gun and fired.

Where the skunk had stood, a hole let daylight through the wooden door. The skunk lay motionless in the gravel in front of the church. He might have lost that battle, but he had won the war. He had let loose a mighty burst of his best perfume just as Gene had pulled the trigger.

It was years before you could go in the church and not catch a whiff of that skunk, especially in the hot, humid days of late summer. It was nearly that long before I could take a bath and not smell skunk in my hair. I didn't get many opportunities to meet any nice, young ladies the rest of that summer. For most of my childhood, every time I saw Gene, he would look at me, smile, and shake his head as if to say, "Them darn city boys. God love 'em, there just ain't no sense in 'em."

CHAPTER 5

"Toss It Back!"

I mentioned earlier that my grandparents were fly-fishers. They were more than just people who fished with a fly rod. They were fly-fishing purists. They believed that any species of fish that swam could and should be caught on a fly rod. Furthermore, any species of fish that swam could be caught on a fly they had tied themselves.

Gramps had gone to what was called "Opening Day" at Bennett Spring State Park on March 1. He had invited me to go along. It was twenty below, cold enough to freeze your tongue to a steel pipe, and I had been afflicted with a bad cold. I respectfully declined. I had never been to an "opener" before and had no idea what all the fuss was about anyway.

A couple of weeks after the skunk episode, Gramps had stopped laughing long enough to ask if I would like to try my hand at fly-fishing for trout. Gramps had a unique way of teaching fly-fishing. He was a firm believer in learning by observation. He would have me watch and then leave me alone to figure it out on my own.

School had been out about a week when Gramps informed me that we would be going fishing at Bennett Spring on Saturday. He had decided that, since my thirteenth birthday was on Saturday, this would make a pretty good birthday present.

I had three days in which to learn how to cast a fly rod and how to use it to catch trout. Gramps gave me an old Heddon three-piece, bamboo fly rod with an automatic reel and level line and proceeded to show me how to cast it. After three or four casts, he handed me the rod, told me to practice, and said he would check on me in an hour.

I stood out there in the middle of the front yard and tried to cast the long, heavy pole. My first attempt had fly line wrapped around my head and shoulders. After fighting with the rod for thirty minutes, I was able to cast the line about twenty feet with some consistency.

At the end of an hour, Gramps came out to watch my cast.

"I showed you the right way to cast that rod. Why are you casting like that? You look like you just stepped in a yellow jacket's nest. This is an art form, not a fly-swatting competition."

He took the rod and showed me again. This time he gave me a couple of hints.

"Stop at one o'clock and let the line straighten out behind you by counting to three. Then cast forward."

After three or four casts, I started to get the feel of the timing.

Gramps smiled and said, "Let's go sit in the shade and talk about some things you need to know."

We sat in lawn chairs under the shade of a Mimosa tree my grandmother had planted thirty years earlier. Gramps and I had used that old Mimosa tree for important business a number of times. I suspected this was going to be important business.

Gramps explained leaders, tippets, stream ethics, and the rules about the number of fish I could keep. We discussed flies and how to present them—dead drifting with nymphs and drag-free floating for dry flies. Most of what he told me went into my ears, swam around in my brain for a second or two, and then disappeared into the black abyss of a twelve-year-old's attention span. *Dead what? Drag race? What the heck does that have to do with fishing for trout?*

The tippet thing made sense. There was no way I was going to remember all those flies and which ones floated and which ones sink. I decided right then and there that, if they were supposed to float, they would. If they were supposed to sink, they would. No big deal there.

After our discussion on the finer points in trout fishing, Gramps stood up and said, "Grab that rod. We need to go down to the pond. You need to learn how to land a fish."

I couldn't believe it. We were going to fish in the pond. I had not had the chance to fish in the pond since I arrived in Missouri. The pond had been frozen over all winter and was now ready for fishing. Truth be known, up to this very point in my young life, I had never been fishing. I had no clue as to what I was about to experience.

Gramps was banging around on the front porch while I opened the gate to the cow pasture. He emerged with a small box, a stringer, and a rusty pair of needle-nose pliers. Gramps didn't believe in walking to the pond when he could drive the pickup. It was only a couple hundred yards, but that was far enough. There were probably a million chiggers and a half a million ticks between the house and the pond. He tossed his handful of fishing implements and a rusty old lawn chair in the back of the truck and drove through the gate. He waited while I reclosed the gate so the cows wouldn't get out, and we were off. Less than a minute later, we were at the pond.

The fishing pond was nestled in a hollow in the woods. It covered about an acre and a half and had an iced-tea color indicative of a wooded pond. Gramps had built a fence around the pond to keep the cows out. He had livestock ponds for them to drink from. This was his exclusive fishing pond, and no cows were allowed.

My shoulder was aching a little from casting that heavy bamboo rod, but I wasn't about to let him know. He showed me how to tie on a fly, actually a small yellow popping bug with tiny black dots. I was ready to fish.

He explained to me that the popping bug would float. I was to cast it out and let it sit motionless until the rings in the water caused by the popping bug landing all disappeared. He told me that it was very important to let the fly sit perfectly still and to raise the rod tip quickly if a fish hit the fly. I wanted to impress my grandfather with my casting, so I concentrated on making the perfect cast.

I made my back cast with just the right amount of energy. I stopped the rod at one o'clock and said to myself, *One, two, three,* and made an attempt to cast the line forward. To my disbelief, I was hung up behind me. I knew I hadn't waited too long. I knew it couldn't be hung on a weed or in the grass. Turning around, I discovered my fly was thirty feet up in a huge white oak tree. With my mouth hanging open, I cautiously glanced over at Gramps.

He was shaking his head but grinning at the same time.

"Boy, what'd I tell you about watchin' your back cast?"

So that was what he meant. I remembered him telling me that but wasn't quite sure why. I would watch my line as it shot out behind me when I was practicing and wondered what I was supposed to be watching for. Now I knew. Gramps was a man of very few words. You had to experience it to understand what he meant sometimes.

He walked over and showed me how to pull the fly out of the tree. He made a point of explaining that you never use the rod to pull a fly out of the leaves or grass or weeds. You always pull directly on the line. If the leader breaks, you tie on another fly. If it doesn't, then no harm is done. If you use the rod, you will probably break the rod before the fly comes loose.

I walked over to the edge of the pond and stripped out some line for another cast. Taking care to avoid the limbs that were hungrily reaching for my fly, I cast the popper out onto the still surface of the pond. I was feeling pretty proud of my cast and turned to see if Gramps had noticed.

As my head turned in his direction, he called out, "Never take your eyes off the fly."

My eyes shot forward at the same instant the water where my popper was sitting exploded, spraying water into the air. By the time my brain registered what was happening, the fish was gone.

"See what I mean?" Gramps called from behind me. "Cast again over by that log. Make sure you set the hook the second the fish hits."

This time my cast went perfectly. The popper dropped within an inch of the log my grandfather had pointed to. The popper wasn't on the water for more than a second when another fish hit. I set the hook and immediately felt the tugging of a fish on the other end. It didn't feel like a big fish, but it was my first fish on a fly rod. I knew my grandfather would be proud of me. I couldn't wait to land it.

I was so excited I started backing up to pull the fish in faster. I tripped over a stick and fell flat on my back. I kept the rod straight up in the air and stripped in the line like a madman. When I stood up, the fish was splashing around in the shallow water at the edge of the pond. It was only about four inches long, but it was a beauty in my eyes.

I reached down to pick up the little bluegill. One of the sharp spines on the dorsal fin pricked my finger as the fish struggled to head into deeper water. You would have thought I had been shot, the way I bellowed in shock and pain. I couldn't believe that little fish hurt my finger. It was really stinging, and there was a tiny drop of blood oozing from my finger. But that wasn't important. I grabbed the line and lifted the fish from the water.

I was the conqueror. It was a bloody battle, but I had won. I held my trophy, the spoils of war, high for my grandfather to see.

"Toss him back!" he ordered.

"What?"

"Toss him back!" he said a little more emphatically.

My grandfather must be out of his mind. This was my first fish on a fly rod. Actually, it was my first fish ever. I took a long last look at the beautiful little fish dangling from my line and removed the hook from its lip. I bent down and released the fish into the water.

I missed seeing it swim away because my eyes were blurred with tears. It would not do for my grandfather to see my eyes wet, so I stood up, wiped my eyes, and purposefully attempted to make another cast.

My posture must have given me away.

I heard him call from behind me, "Son. Come over here for a minute."

I reeled in my line and turned toward him, looking down so he wouldn't see my eyes. He was sitting on an old tree stump and motioned for me to sit down in the rickety lawn chair beside him. I dragged my feet, pouted, and huffed over to the chair. I flopped down and waited for what he had to say.

When I looked into his face, I saw something I rarely saw in him. There was a soft compassion in his eyes. I almost welled up again.

"That was your very first fish, wasn't it?" I nodded without saying a word.

"It was a feisty little guy, wasn't it?" I nodded once again.

"I noticed it finned you when you first tried to handle it. Smarts, don't it?"

Once again I nodded and looked at my finger. The redness was gone, as was the pain.

"There's a trick to handlin' spiny finned fish. You need to slide your hand from the head toward the tail down along their top fin, that's called the dorsal fin, and lay the dorsal fin down as you wrap your fingers around it. They won't fin you that way. When you're holding the fish, you need to remember not to squeeze too hard. That'll hurt 'em and maybe even kill 'em. Do you know why I told you to turn it loose?"

I whimpered a pathetic "No."

He sat there quiet for a minute, staring at the pond and thinking about what he was going to say next.

"That fish was just a baby. There are adult bluegills in this here pond that are larger and ready for eatin'. That one wouldn't have made the skillet stink. In a couple of years, it will grow to be quite the fighter and make a good meal. When you caught that one, you gave it an education. It's kind of like the first time you burnt your finger on something hot. You may not remember when you did, but you know now not to touch things that are hot. That fish may not remember what just happened, but it will be much more selective about what it tries to put in its mouth. It has an instinct for survival, and that instinct will help it to learn from its mistakes. It will be a while before you catch that one again. That's why it will have a chance to grow to be a big fish one day. Someday it will forget and grab another one of your flies. By then it will be big enough to give you a good fight and a good meal. That's all we can expect from a bluegill. Do you understand what I'm sayin'?"

I thought about what my grandfather had said.

"Gramps, what if someone else catches it?"

He looked at me and smiled. "That one is yours to catch. You turned it loose. Mother Nature'll insist that you be the one to catch it again someday. It's important that we turn some of the fish we catch back to be caught again. If we don't, someday there won't be any to catch. Do you understand?"

My twelve-year-old brain really did comprehend. That talk has stuck with me my entire life and followed me down my chosen path. Be careful what you say to a kid. You might just turn him into a catch-and-release advocate.

CHAPTER 6

Santa's Magic Is Found to Be Wanting

The deliciously acrid scent of oak wood smoke wafted gently in the air as Gramps poked at the fire with the stove poker.

"Stop messing with the stove, Gramps. You'll put the fire out," Granny said in her usual fun-but-fussy tone.

She always accused Gramps of being able to put out a house fire with a stove poker. I sleepily glanced from the TV over to where Gramps stood bent over, poking at the fire in the *Warm Morning* woodburning stove.

I listened impatiently, trying to hear the soft hiss of snow falling between the clanks of the steel stove poker and the television turned up loudly for my hard-of-hearing grandparents. It was December 23, 1967, and everything was perfect for a white Christmas and a cherished memory. I hope Granny remembered to tell Santa (Gramps) that I wanted a guitar this year.

Without warning, the brain-fogging aroma of roasting turkey forced my stomach to growl loudly in anticipation. The mouth-watering titillation of cinnamon and nutmeg steeped in pumpkin, baking at a perfect 350 degrees, forced another overly noisy growl from my constantly starving stomach. I fought hard to push all thoughts of

food aside as I contemplated the most important event, the impend-
ing arrival of Santa Claus and his eight flying reindeer. Even though
I was too old to still believe in Santa Clause, I knew with all my heart
they were on a mission with one purpose, to bring me a brand-new
guitar so perfectly made it could play the latest and hottest sounds
all by itself.

Comfort and warmth took hold of my eyelids while I laid in
bed covered by three heavy, handmade quilts snuggled deeply into an
old-fashioned, feather-down, tick mattress. Coalie, my dog, always
slept under the covers at my feet. I don't know how she breathed
under there, but she sure did do a great job of keeping my feet warm.
The plans I was making to hold rock concerts and be adored by
throngs of screaming girls started to jumble as sleep came. Tomorrow
was Christmas Eve. A deep sigh slipped from my lips as I turned onto
my side and drifted into a black abyss.

Coalie snorted and rooted her way from under the covers at my
feet to emerge by my face. A wet tongue slid along my closed left eye,
announcing it was time to wake up. I wiped at my eye and gave her a
hug just before she leapt to the cold hardwood floor of my bedroom.
I could hear her toenails clicking on the floor as she made her way to
the bedroom door.

The door was always open just a crack to allow some of the
heat from the wood stove to keep my bedroom from becoming a
deepfreeze. Coalie had a routine. She would claw at the door to open
it just far enough to get her wet nose through the crack. She would
push the door wide open and then head straight for the kitchen,
where she knew Granny would have a chopped-up fried egg waiting
in her food bowl along with a cup of Hound Dog dry dog food.
Coalie had a fried egg for breakfast every day of her eighteen-year
life. Consequently, she had the shiniest black coat of fur covering her
portly build you have ever seen on a dog.

Coalie was mostly dachshund but had something else in her
because she was a little large for that breed. She was completely black
except for a small white patch on her chest. Because of her eating
habits, she was enough overweight that, when she sat and looked up
at you, she looked a lot like a shiny black seal begging for a fish.

She was a great dog for a boy. She went everywhere with me—except to school, of course. She would tag along when I went squirrel hunting and sometimes even tree a squirrel. She never ran away scared when I shot my .22 rifle, and never, ever chased the cows. A dog that chased cows was a dog whose life span was shortened around our place.

I crawled out from under the warmth of the quilts and sat up. I gingerly tested the floor with one toe and decided I would not turn into a popsicle if I put both feet down on it. Rubbing the sleep from my eyes, I made my way to the bathroom to wash the sleep from my face and comb my hair. Granny had standards about appearance at the breakfast table. What I saw in the mirror was not acceptable by her standards. After brushing my teeth and combing my hair, I made some faces at myself in the mirror and went back to the bedroom to get dressed. No school today; it was Christmas Eve. Even so, the cows needed to be fed, so I put on my work clothes and headed for the kitchen.

Granny handed me a biscuit with a sausage patty in the middle and pushed me out the door, saying, "Gramps is out loading the hay. You better get a move on, young man!"

I stuffed the entire biscuit and sausage into my mouth and ran out the door. The cold air nearly knocked me back inside. I glanced at the large thermometer hanging on the side of the house. It showed a frigid thirteen degrees. Man, that was too cold to be out feeding the cows.

When I complained to Gramps after reaching the barn, he mentioned that, maybe if I lived outside with the cows for a while, I might get used to it. I knew that I would never get used to being outside all the time in thirteen-degree temperatures and said so. He looked at me and smiled.

"The cows never get used to it either. The hay they eat is what keeps them alive in this cold weather. If it's too cold for man, it's too cold for the beast. Let's get these poor old cows fed and go see what Granny has for breakfast."

We finished loading up the hay bales in the little trailer Gramps pulled behind the 1948 Ford model 8N tractor and drove out into the snow-covered pasture. The cows followed us in a long line of black, mooing their need for nourishment.

My job was to ride with the hay, cut the strings on the bales, and drop off flakes of the hay bales as we drove. This way, we would leave a long line of hay hunks for the cows to eat, so every cow had its own flake of hay. Gramps said they would not waste as much that way. Any uneaten hay made a warm bed for some of the calves to lie in while their mommas chewed their cud.

Once the last of the hay was dropped, Gramps turned in the tractor seat and started to count the cows. I started counting as well. I had learned that he would always finish counting with the question, "How many d'you count?" I knew I had to be ready with a number. It had better match Gramps's number, or we would be there, counting cows all day until they matched.

I couldn't help but feel sorry for the old cows. They stood there in the freezing cold, munching on dried-up hunks of grass, not much of a breakfast by my standards. Our cows were all black. We raised registered Black Angus cattle. That day, though, our black cows had white backs. The snow had frozen to the hair on their backs. Some even had small icicles hanging from the edge of their nostrils, forming as their moist breath bellowed out as a white vapor each time they exhaled. To me, they were the epitome of the word *miserable*. However, they seemed perfectly content to stand hock deep in snow, chewing on hay and murmuring low moos of contentment to each other.

After feeding the cows, we still had a little work to do. We drove the tractor and trailer up to the garage/shop and threw an ax and a shovel in the trailer. We drove back out into the pasture and made tracks for the livestock pond. Once there, I grabbed the shovel, and Gramps picked up the double-bit ax. Gramps would not use his good ax for chopping ice. The ax designated for that job was a rusted piece of iron so dull, accidentally cutting off a toe would be a major feat.

Gramps would chop a hole in the ice about two-feet square and then break the big chunk of ice floating in the hole into small pieces. My job was to scoop out the small chunks of ice, making a nice, clean hole for the cows to drink from. If you didn't get most of the ice chunks out of the hole, it would freeze back over before the cows could get a drink. If a cow touched its nose to ice, no matter how thin it might be, it would not push hard enough to break the ice for a drink and go off wandering in search of water.

We didn't want them to wander out onto the pond. There was the danger of breaking through or falling on the ice and not being able to get up. Eventually their body warmth would melt the ice, and the cow would fall through. Either scenario was a bad one. Once we opened up a dozen holes we proceeded to the house.

My nose and hands felt as if they had been immersed in liquid nitrogen; if I hit them, they would shatter into a million pieces. I stood in front of the wood stove and warmed my legs, butt, and hands until Granny called out to "come and get it."

After breakfast, Gramps and I went out to the shop to "potter" around, mostly to get out from under Granny's feet while she prepared Christmas Day–dinner fixins'. We were expecting company. My cousins, Dee and Sue, and their mom and dad were joining us for Christmas. They were due to arrive from Kansas in a couple of hours. Dee was a nickname given to my cousin Stanley. Stanley Keaton III, or Dee the Turd as we liked to call him, he acquired the nickname, "Dee," because his buzz-cut hairstyle showed the profile of his head, which formed a perfect letter D. He must have spent his entire baby years lying on his back. His head was completely flat in back. He was four years younger than me, but we had a great time playing together when he came to visit.

Sue was my age and a tomboy. She played just as hard at cops and robbers, or cowboys and Indians, as we did.

Gramps and I were busy in the garage when the bird dogs, Suzie and Lightning the English Setters, started barking up a storm. I ran up to the house in time to see Dee and Sue pile out of the back seat of their dad's '65 Ford Comet. It was a mint-red-and-white, shiny, chrome-encrusted work of art that any thirteen year-old boy would give up his favorite fishing pole for. What a great-looking car!

I hadn't seen Dee and Sue in over a year and was astonished at the changes. Dee had let his hair grow a little longer (actually, his mom and dad allowed him to grow it longer, if the truth be known) and you couldn't see the D shape of his head. And Sue! Whoa! Sue had started turning into a real girl. It looked like she might actually be wearing a bra. She was wearing a dress. She would have to change before she could play with Dee and me. We didn't have time for girls in dresses.

Dee and I spent the day playing in the house, driving Sue crazy with our boy pranks, and getting under Granny's feet way too often.

After a meal worthy of the three kings in the Baby Jesus story and some severe scolding to hold the noise down to a low roar, it was time for bed. Santa was coming (Dee still believed), and we were pretty wound up. I tossed and turned, trying to fall asleep. I just knew that Santa was going to bring the guitar I wanted. This guitar would be the one that would play itself, rocketing me to instant fame as a rock-and-roll star. *Look out, world. A new Jimmy Hendrix is in the making!* I slipped into sleep as the roar of the stadium filled with screaming fans died to a hush as I hit the first chord on my brand-new electric guitar.

The first chord I played sounded like the lost chord from heaven in a perfect harmonious vibration and then changed to a sound like Dee's voice, telling me to get up because Santa had been here. I sat straight up in bed and opened my eyes as wide as I could to show him I was awake.

"Have you been out there yet?" I asked.

"Yeah, and there are presents everywhere. Come on, man, let's go see what we got."

"Is anyone else awake?"

He shook his head and motioned toward the door. We crept from the bedroom as quiet as mice. We slipped into the living room where the Christmas tree stood tall and delightfully laden with blinking lights and sweet candy canes. I had eyes for one thing and one thing only. I did not see it. There was no guitar standing, laying, or hanging anywhere in the room. My heart sank. *This is going to be the worst Christmas ever.* I watched sadly as Dee poked, shook, and dropped every package under the tree. He made enough noise that the house began to awaken. Granny walked into the living room on her way to the kitchen and told us to stay out of the presents until after breakfast. Normally, I would have moaned and complained about having to wait until after breakfast. Today I just didn't care. No guitar meant no Christmas in my book.

After breakfast, I provided the obligatory smile when handed a package from my aunt and uncle. *Wow, a pair of socks! Man did I need them. Thanks!* I sat with a face as long as a horse's until all the packages were distributed and in the process of being gleefully torn apart by Dee and Sue. I sat pouting as I looked at the pair of socks, a bottle of Old Spice aftershave, and a package of Fruit of the Loom briefs piled in front of me on the floor. Boy, I must not have been as good this year as I thought I had.

Gramps stood up and said, "I almost forgot. I think Santa left one more present, and for some reason, he put it in my room. Hold on while I get it."

He must have gotten Granny something pretty special for him to hide it in his room, I thought to myself. Gramps walked in with the weirdest-looking package I had ever seen. It was shaped like an elongated diamond. It was more like two triangles put together end to end. It was about four feet long and two-feet wide at the widest section in the middle.

Granny clapped her hands together and asked what Gramps had gotten her. Gramps told her that the name on the package was not hers. At that, my ears suddenly turned on and began sweeping in his direction like two satellite dishes homing in on some extraterrestrial message from space.

"I'm not sure, but I think it says to Mark from Santa on the tag here, Granny. I wonder what this strange-looking present is?"

With that, he handed the present to me. I reached up and gingerly took it from his hands. A smile began to form on my face against my will as I held this amazing gift. I just couldn't keep it from happening. I could feel cracks forming on both cheeks as the stone veneer began to crumble away. The box was long enough and weighed just the right amount to be a guitar. I tore into the wrapping paper with renewed life and a renewed faith in Old Saint Nick. *I do believe, I do believe,* I thought to myself.

There on the box was a picture of a guitar. It was a guitar! It was! I couldn't believe it. It really was a guitar! I carefully opened the box and slipped the plastic bag off the most beautiful thing I had ever seen in my life. The name on the head was Stella. To me she would always be my Stella. She had six strings that shined like brand-new nickels. Her face was a deep burgundy blending into a black strum board. There were mock mother-of-pearl inlays up and down the neck of my Stella. I was in love.

I carefully assumed the position and cradled her like I had seen all the stars on television do. I held her neck with my left hand and prepared to play her like no one had ever played a guitar before. My fingers strummed hard against the six strings and produced the most...awful sound my young ears had ever heard. I tried it again and again, but all I could get out of her were terrible sounds that reminded me of the sounds the cats in the barn made in February when they are making kittens.

"Gonna have to make him a practice room on the back forty, Granny," Gramps said, chuckling.

Practice? What does he mean, practice? I thought these things just made beautiful music no matter who played them. After about ten minutes of trying to make a perfect chord, my fingers where getting sore trying to hold down certain strings like it showed in the book that came with the guitar. I began to realize that I might not be the rock star I had hoped to be by the time school started back after Christmas vacation. Santa had fallen way short on his magic this year.

I would have my time in the limelight as a rock-and-roll star for a brief couple of months, as a foursome of my high-school buddies and I formed a band. We called ourselves Uncle Sam's Draft Bait Band and played mostly Creedence Clearwater Revival songs. I never did master the guitar. I played the saxophone and was only moderately decent at it. I lasted in the band for about half of a school year. I really didn't have much talent in the music field. I would discover that my talent was in the field of fly-fishing. That was where, if ever, I would find my fame and, uh, not much in the way of fortune.

CHAPTER 7

"Whistle? What Whistle?"

Sleep was an elusive wisp of smoke. I laid in the dark, imagining monster trout taking my fly. My mind raced. I rehearsed all that I could remember from the lessons Gramps had taught me over the last three days. Which knot did I use to tie on the fly? It was the clinch, wasn't it? When my grandmother opened the bedroom door to awaken me, I felt as if I had been asleep for only a few minutes. As I slid out from under the covers, blackness outside my window confused my sleep-deprived brain. I knew I was going trout fishing with my grandfather, but I wasn't sure if my grandmother knew what time it was. It was still night outside.

When I emerged from the bathroom, I saw my grandfather sitting at the table, sipping a steaming cup of coffee. My olfactory senses were just starting to cut through my sleep-heavy brain. I smelled something familiar. It was a combination of wood smoke, fresh coffee, and fried bacon. *Ahh!* I thought with a sigh, *Heaven.* There was nothing like that smell. It brought thoughts of warmth, contentment, and a slice of excitement for the adventure of a new day.

Granny was in the kitchen, loading an old-fashioned stainless-steel cooler with cold fried chicken, wedges of homemade apple pie, a hunk of Colby cheese, a quart mason jar filled with sweetened iced tea, and some biscuits slathered in butter and molasses. She added a half gallon milk carton filled with water and frozen solid to keep everything cold—a lunch fit for a pair of trout-fishing kings.

Gramps began to gather fishing gear: his new fishing vest, his old fishing vest (for me), two fly rods and reels, the old-style gut leaders he had started soaking last night, stringers, and landing nets. Finally, he brought out a couple pairs of chest waders. Mine were hand-me-downs just like the vest. The waders Gramps had given me were the old rubber style with bicycle-tire patches stuck everywhere. They looked like one of Granny's piecework quilts.

By the time we had all the gear and the cooler loaded, the clock was showing 4:00 a.m. Bennett Spring was only forty-five miles from the farm, but we had to allow time for buying the daily tag, getting geared up, and finding the right spot before someone else got it. All of this could have been done with an hour and a half to spare except for one additional factor. Gramps didn't like to drive over forty miles an hour going downhill. His average speed was usually closer to about twenty miles an hour.

"Those damn teenagers drivin' like bats outa heck will be the death of us all."

Gramps figured anybody under the age of fifty was a teenager and wasn't experienced enough to be driving anyway.

We stood a few feet apart in the ice-cold stream. I tried to focus on the streambank directly across from me in the darkness just prior to sunrise. It never got any darker than that. I couldn't even see the end of my fly rod. Gramps had told me not to start fishing until the whistle blew. Who could fish? I couldn't see where I was, let alone make a cast to a fish in that black void. I stood there, shivering in the cold, predawn air, waiting for that dang whistle. There were anglers lined up along the stream side by side, whispering and planning their strategies for catching the big one they saw last week.

After what seemed like hours, a slight brightening in the sky made it possible to see the other side of the stream. What I saw next caused me to gasp. I looked to my left and then to my right. There were anglers lined up along the stream, elbow to elbow, for a mile in both directions. There had to be thousands of them. This was going to be a madhouse when that danged whistle finally took a notion to blow. Who was going to blow it anyway? How in the world were people all the way down on the other end going to hear that stupid whistle? Man, I was getting cold. My fingers didn't have any feeling in them. I was pretty sure I had been paralyzed from the knees down from the cold water seeping into my leaking waders. *There's no way I'm going to catch a fish with this many fisherman here. There couldn't be that many fish in this stream.*

About the time I was thinking of telling Gramps to call an ambulance, a reverberation erupted with such an ear-splitting siren sound; I thought someone had tried to fish before the whistle, and the cops were about to arrest him right then and there. At the same instant, everybody on the stream started casting. It must be some sort of comradely act or something. If everybody started fishing before the whistle, they couldn't arrest all of us. I just stood there, flabbergasted.

Even Gramps was in on it. He looked over at me and asked, "Didn't you hear the whistle?"

How in the world did he hear that whistle with that loud siren going off? Oh! That was the whistle? Maybe he could have warned me that it was actually a siren. Another lesson in taking things these country folks say too literally.

People were fighting fish all around me. Gramps already had a nice trout on when I made my first cast. Because there were so many people fishing so close, my first cast ended up tangled in the line of the guy next to me. He patiently waited while I untangled the mess I had made and went right back to fishing without a word.

On my next cast, the fly of choice hit the water about two feet in front of me. I looked at Gramps, hoping he had not seen that cast. He was too busy landing another fish. I quickly recovered and cast again. The line rolled out beautifully! The fly began to sink, and I felt a strong tug on the end of the line. I set the hook, and the fight was on... for about two seconds. *Shoot! It got off.*

I cast again and started stripping the black-and-yellow marabou streamer back toward me. Something grabbed my line and nearly jerked the rod right out of my hand. I set the hook, and this time I gave it an extra tug to make sure the hook was set. The fish fought hard, but I kept him on. It would run and strip out line and then pause for a breather. I would quickly retrieve the line the rainbow had taken off my reel. Back and forth we fought. I got more and more excited with each minute that went by. Finally, I was ready to land my fish.

I reached around to my back where my net was hanging. Before I could find it, I noticed my grandfather standing next to me with his net sliding through the water and under my fish as skillfully as a surgeon. He scooped it up and let out a whoop!

"Nice trout! Not bad for your first trout. Gotta weigh in at a strong three pounds!"

Other anglers were looking at my fish, oohing and aahing. Gramps beamed with pride as he announced that his grandson had caught that monster. He had taught that boy everything he knew. Gramps helped me string the fish and gave me a few tidbits of information to file in my arsenal of fish-catching secrets.

The memories of that day are still crystal clear even forty-plus years later as I sit here remembering them. We fished together until eleven o'clock and stopped to devour that scrumptious lunch Granny had packed. We each had four of the five fish we were allowed for the day. We cleaned our fish and put them in the cooler with that still-frozen milk jug. Gramps and I sat at a picnic table and discussed the fish to that point. Each of us had caught and released several. Gramps had released nearly twenty. I had released ten. We could only keep one more. We decided to go catch our last fish and call it a day. I hadn't noticed the aching in my shoulder caused by the heavy bamboo fly rod while I was catching fish. After lunch and a little rest, the ache was getting serious. Besides that, I couldn't wait to get home to show Granny my big three-pounder!

Gramps had his last fish five minutes after we walked back to the stream. I fished for another thirty minutes with no luck. Gramps had helped me out with some different flies for a while and then decided to take a nap under a big white oak. He leaned his rod against the tree, sat down beside it, and rested his back against its rough bark. He was snoring in less time than it took me to make my next cast. I gave up in another hour. That last fish just wasn't going to cooperate.

I was cold, wet, my shoulder felt like someone had ripped it out of my socket and beat me with it, and I was anxious to sample whatever goodies Granny would have for supper. I woke up Gramps and told him I wanted to go home. He asked me if I had caught that last fish.

"No, I decided I would leave him till next time. He will be waiting just for me because I had let him go this time."

Gramps smiled and nodded. We loaded up our gear and headed down the road toward home, warm, dry clothes and a "Granny" supper. There's nothing finer.

I slept on the way home. Dreams of aqua blue filled my vision. Black silhouettes in the shape of very large rainbow trout swam into view opening their mouths and engulfing my fly. I jerked so hard when I set the hook I woke myself up. I looked over at Gramps. He had a pleased smile on his face as he stared straight ahead, minding his driving.

CHAPTER 8

Our Neurotic Roosters

Gramps had been patiently trying to teach me the fine art of fly-tying off and on since my first trip to Bennett Spring. I was getting pretty good at tying a fly that looked like something. Probably not what it was supposed to be, but something resembling something that could accidentally, on a dark night, look like a fly. The second stage of a budding fly tier is what I like to call the creative stage. The first stage being the "I don't have a clue what I'm doing" stage.

I was cranking out totally useless, but cool-looking, flies by the dozens. One evening while tying a fly that resembled a cross between a woolly worm and a Chihuahua, Gramps commented on how few feathers he had. He looked at the creation in my vise, and muttered something about weird concoctions, and told me that Saturday was "Plucking Day," and I had better be available about six o'clock in the evening.

He left the room before my brain registered what he said. Plucking Day? What the heck was Plucking Day? *If I tie in this bright-red piece of yarn right here and fold it just so...*

I had eaten enough supper to feed an army of boys my age. All I wanted to do was go sit in the recliner and watch TV until the uncomfortable, overstuffed feeling around my beltline dissipated. That second piece of homemade apple pie was the straw that broke the camel's back, but hey, it was Saturday night, and nothing was going on. I didn't even have any homework.

Gramps got up from the table, went into the kitchen, and reappeared with a brown paper grocery bag in his hand.

"Mark, go fetch a wire clothes hanger and meet me at the chicken house."

I had no clue what he was up to. Getting up out of the recliner, I had just plopped into was as hard a work as I had hoped to deal with this evening. I scrounged around in the hall closet and found a wire hanger and headed out to the chicken house. What was Gramps going to do with a paper bag and a clothes hanger? He came out of the garage, adding another piece to this mysterious puzzle. He had a pair of pliers along with the paper bag. My curiosity was about to cause an aneurysm

"What are we doing, Gramps?"

"Remember I told you that today was Plucking Day?"

This time I noticed that he uttered those words, "Plucking Day," with some sort of hushed reverence. It was almost as if he was talking in the library or was afraid someone would hear him. He put his finger to his lips, signaling me to be quiet.

He motioned for me to hand him the coat hanger. I watched as he untwisted the part of the hanger that looked like a hook. He then proceeded to straighten the hanger out. It looked as if he was getting ready to open a locked car door with an Arkansas door key. He used pliers to bend the end of the hanger into a small, tight hook.

He whispered to me as he stood just outside the chicken-house door. It was late enough in the evening that the chickens were all on the roost.

"You know that ginger-colored rooster of mine?"

I nodded an affirmative.

"You are going to slip inside the chicken house, find that rooster, take this here hanger, and slip the hooked end around his leg. Be sure to hook him above the spur. That'll keep him from slipping out of the hook. As soon as you hook him, pull him off the roost and grab him under your arm like you would carry a football. Then step out here where I'll be waitin'."

I stared at Gramps like he was nuts. I opened and closed my mouth like a fish out of water, but no words came out.

He looked straight at me and said, "You used up all the good feathers. You have to help me get some more."

Gramps had three roosters specifically pampered for their feathers. One was a beautiful black-and-white grizzly, which he called a "dominicker," one had the best-looking ginger neck and saddle feathers I have ever seen, and the other was just plain old black. Rooster feathers generally weren't worth a darn until the rooster reached at least two years old. Gramps had been harvesting feathers from this trio of spurs and beaks for a couple of years already. This put their age somewhere in the neighborhood of four years.

I didn't know we were just taking a few feathers. I couldn't believe Gramps was going to kill a rooster that I knew for a fact he pampered for some feathers. I took the wire hanger converted into an implement of death and opened the chicken-house door. I stepped inside the dusty darkness and waited for my eyes to adjust. I could vaguely make out the rows of chickens sitting on the three-tiered roosts. As my eyes adjusted to the darkness, I could see the large grizzly rooster sitting next to the black one. Just to the right of the black one was the ginger rooster.

I eased in for a closer look. Yep, that was him. I carefully slipped the wire hook under him. I could see better now. He stood up like he was ready to fly off the roost. I was able to make out the very sharp, pointed, two-inch spur on the side of his leg. If you have ever been flogged by a mad rooster with two-inch spurs, you learn to respect them. Those spurs at eye level made me nervous.

The rooster was starting to act goosey. I knew I had to act quickly and decisively. I pulled hard and snagged the rooster off of the roost. Wings where flapping, chickens were squawking, and chicken-house dust filled my mouth and nose. I folded the rooster's wings in against his body and tucked him under my arm like a football. I stepped out into the night air and breathed deeply of its damp freshness. Gramps was standing there with his brown paper bag and a flashlight he pulled from his pocket.

I had no idea how he planned to "do the hit" on this rooster with a brown paper bag.

"Bring him over here and hold on tight to him. Watch out for those saddle feathers. Don't mess 'em up," Gramps demanded.

I eased over to him slowly. Dread filled my soul. I could feel the rapid beat of the rooster's heart and realized I didn't want any part of the terrible event about to take place.

"Gramps," I said tentatively, "do we hafta kill it?"

"Kill it? Nah! These are the best darned roosters in the county for fly-tying feathers. We're not gonna kill it. We're gonna pluck out a few feathers to tie with."

"What? You mean we're gonna pull out their feathers by the roots and not kill 'em?"

I thought that might be crueler than just offing the bird right there and now.

Gramps smiled and said, "Yep. That way we can have good feathers for as long as this here bird is alive. They grow back new ones."

At that, Gramps plucked a small bundle of two or three feathers from the neck of his prized ginger rooster. The rooster didn't seem as upset with the process as I thought it would. One at a time we harvested feathers from each of his three roosters.

One little detail that slipped my grandfather's mind was that it would not be a good idea for either him or me to get too close to any of the roosters for the next week or so, as I would soon learn.

The next morning, Granny asked me to feed the chickens. Unaware of the sinister plot being hatched by the "Tres Amigos," I sauntered into the chicken pen with a bucket of cracked corn and laying pellets. All at once, I was blinded by flapping wings and felt a tearing sting in my shin. I turned to run out of the pen when a flurry of ginger-colored feathers began to beat me, and a sharp, two-inch-long spur just missed taking out my right eye.

I was swatting the air like hornets were after me. I stumbled and clawed my way to the gate. Before I could turn the wooden button to open the gate, the black rooster decided to take his turn on me. He was a much better marksman with his spurs. While flogging me with his wings, he attacked my shin over and over with his sharp weapons. I don't know how I did it, but I managed to escape through the gate and slam it shut behind me. Tears welled up in my eyes as the shock began to fade to reality. I was bleeding, sweating, swearing, and crying all at the same time. I ran into the house, yelling for my granny. The look of horror on her face made me burst into downright sobs. She rushed over and guided me to a chair in the kitchen and started asking what had happened.

Granny listened as I retold the story. One time I looked up from explaining my plight and noticed Gramps in the front room. He quickly exited to his room. I could have sworn he was laughing. As the humiliation of having the crap kicked out of me by some dumb roosters took hold, I stopped crying and hung my head in shame. I heard Gramps in the back bedroom. He was splitting a gut, laughing so hard. Granny was doing a little better. Every time she looked at me, she would start to laugh and then stifle it.

Granny finally told me to go to the bathroom and clean up for breakfast. I stared in the mirror for a moment. There in front of me was an image that would bring a laugh to even the sternest of men. I had chicken feathers in my hair and hanging on my lip. My face was black from sweat and dust, stirred up by those darned, mean roosters. Chicken manure on my shoulder depicted the final act of humiliation heaped on me by those winged demons. There were two round holes in my dirt-caked face where I had rubbed the tears away. I looked a lot like a coon that had just got caught robbing the chicken coop.

The feathers were grown back before I went anywhere near that chicken coop again. Thereafter, I was much more conservative with feathers. The price I paid for those feathers was just too darned high.

CHAPTER 9

Rube's Special Melons

One of the most colorful characters I have ever had the privilege to know was an old-timer named Rube. Rube was a tall, five feet five inches, and built like a bantam (pronounced "Banty" in the Ozarks) rooster. Bantam roosters carried themselves with a high degree of self-confidence and an air that said, "I will fight anyone twice my size anytime." Rube struck me as having that same air, though I never saw or heard of him fighting anyone.

He did tell me a story of going out to the west coast to pick fruit during the depression days. He told me that he would wear a thin silk shirt on pay day and walk around some of the toughest areas he knew of with a large roll of toy money rolled up in his shirt pocket. He just wanted to see if anyone would fall for it and try to take it away from him.

Rube had three claims to fame. The first was his hand-carved walking sticks. He was a true artist with a sharp penknife and a stick of hickory. He could carve a walking stick that looked like a wooden chain. I watched him carve beautiful filigree in the handle of a walking stick. Inside the handle was a round wooden ball. The ball was carved from the outside and left to roll around inside the handle. As you can imagine, this thirteen-year-old was totally impressed.

Rube's second claim to fame was his watermelon patch. Rube grew the best red-and-yellow-meat watermelons you ever put in your mouth (my favorites were the yellow-meat melons). They were juicy, firm, and had just the right amount of sweetness. After chilling in a cold spring for a day, the crisp sweetness of Rube's melons could make a grown man cry for more.

Rube's final, and probably most significant, contribution to mankind was his fine moonshine. Rube had a progressive policy for selling his shine. If Rube had placed a shingle out front, it would have said, "If you are old enough to ask for it, you are old enough to buy it."

I first heard about Rube's special elixir of the gods when I was thirteen and a half. That half was pretty important when you weren't quite fourteen. Well, it was almost half.

The harvest of watermelons was in full swing when I overheard some of the older boys in the community talking about Rube's "special melons." My curiosity finally got the best of me. I knew Rube's melons were special. It was just the way those boys were talking. I knew they were discussing something that their parents wouldn't be too proud of.

The low, hushed, and excited tones were a dead giveaway.

I finally asked, "So what in the name of great watermelons are you guys talking about?"

The boys all looked at me like I was some sort of alien.

"You don't know about Rube's special melons?"

I shook my head. I could tell by the tone of the question that I was about to be tagged the village idiot.

"Yeah, well, I know some things you don't."

"Like what?" retorted one on the meanest of the group

"Like how Rube can carve a wooden ball inside a walking stick."

"That ain't nuttin'." That reply came from Jimmy Dade. He was the oldest kid in the senior high-school class. I think he was almost twenty. "Rube's special melons got one heck of a kick in 'em. Am bettin' you can't walk straight after just one bite of them there special melons."

Jimmy was a pretty good guy. He just took a little longer to learn than most. He did seem to get into trouble his fair share of the time too. I looked right in to those eyes of Jimmy's and saw fear. Mine! It was so bright it reflected right back at me. I was afraid to take him up on this implied dare, and I was afraid not to.

"I bet I could," I said a little too weakly for my taste.

Jimmy and the rest of the boys let out a chorus of hoots and guffaws.

"Yeah right!" they all said at the same time.

"I bet I could," I insisted.

I was beginning to wonder just what the heck I was so adamantly proclaiming I could do. I had no idea what these boys where talking about. Of course, I would never let them know.

Jimmy looked sharply at me and looked around like he was going to tell a very secret, secret. After looking to his right and then to his left, he leaned forward, grabbed me by the shirt front, and pulled me close to his face. His breath smelled like the inside of an ash tray. Jimmy tightened his lips into two thin, pale lines.

"All right, you little twerp, be at the old Flesher-place bridge this Saturday 'round two. We'll just see if yuns is man 'nough to eat one o' Rube's special melons."

I had to think fast. Was I supposed to do something on Saturday? I hoped so. My mind scrambled for an excuse. It couldn't find one.

"Okay! I'll be there. And you better be there too with one of those special melons."

I couldn't believe I said that to Jimmy. He just smiled an intimidating-looking smile and slapped one of his groupies on the back of the head as he and his cronies walked away.

I stood rooted in place for a few minutes, wondering what I had just gotten into. I saw Donald Ray, my best friend, standing about ten feet away. He was staring at me and looking very pale.

"Man, I thought ol' Jimmy was gonna kill you or sumpin'. What was he whispering to you about?"

I struggled to get my mouth to work. "He dared me to eat one bite of one of Rube's special melons and then be able to walk." I guess the questioning look in my eyes was clear enough.

"You don't know about Rube's special melons, do ya?"

I looked behind me to make sure Jimmy was way out of earshot.

"No," I replied quietly. "What the heck is Jimmy talking about?"

Donald Ray hesitated for a moment, thinking about the best way to cushion the blow.

"You do know that Rube is a moonshiner, don't cha?"

I had heard that mentioned. I didn't know what it meant. I guess I just thought it meant that he liked to go out at night partying or something.

"Yeah, so?"

"Well, Rube puts 'shine in his melons."

I was getting more confused by the minute. This sounded like some supernatural superstition to me. How do you put the light of the moon in a watermelon? I decided the only way to get a straight answer was to admit that I didn't know what the heck Donald Ray was talking about.

"Start from the beginning. What does it mean to be a moonshiner?"

Donald Ray looked at me in total disbelief. Remembering that I had only lived in the "country" for ten months, he had some semblance of compassion for my ignorance.

"Moonshine is homemade whiskey," he said

Wow! What a revelation that was. I was so far off base I wasn't even in the same ballpark.

"So Rube puts his homemade whiskey in a watermelon?"

"Yep! That what's meant by his special melons."

Now it was starting to make a little sense. I had tasted whiskey back in the city the first time when one of my gang brothers had stolen some from a liquor store. It tasted terrible. But it was the cool thing to do. After a while, I got used to its bitter taste. Wait a minute! I had just agreed to eat a watermelon with whiskey in it. *My granny is going to kill me! Granny was a church going tea totaler.*

Saturday came way too fast. I had been dreading this day since Jimmy made that dare on Tuesday. The walk to the old Flesher place, where a low-water bridge spanned my favorite creek was about a mile. I used that entire mile trying to figure out a way to get out of this dare. I simply could not come up with anything that sounded plausible. When I reached the bottom of a long hill, the river bottom spread out before me. About a hundred yards away, I could see Jimmy and a couple other guys standing on the bridge, smoking cigarettes. Jimmy saw me coming and waved me over. I heard a car coming down the road behind me, so I stepped off the road and waited for it to go by. Donald Ray pulled up in his old pickup truck and stopped.

"I figured you wouldn't back out," he called through the driver's side window. "Hop in."

I ran around the truck and got in. Maybe Donald Ray had a great plan to get me out of this predicament.

"You got any ideas on what I should do?"

"Yep."

"What?"

"Don't eat too much of that melon, or Granny'll skin yer hide."

We pulled to a stop on the shoulder of the gravel road at the bridge. I got out of the truck, stuck out my chest, and stood as tall as I could.

I walked over to Jimmy and said, "Where's that melon?"

"I didn't think you'd show up, city boy," Jimmy half smiled, half snarled.

Jimmy's cronies were chanting something about the land of fruits and nuts as a backup chorus behind him.

"Well, you was wrong. I'm here, and I'm ready."

Jimmy slipped over the side of the bridge and fished a melon out of the water. He pulled a long pocketknife from the pocket of his jeans and sliced off the end of the melon. He cut a chunk out of the melon's heart and handed me a fist-sized piece.

"If you eat all of that there piece and can still walk in ten minutes, I'd be surprised!"

I took a tentative bite. It tasted sweeter than usual but had no bad taste to it. I noticed something different too. It was sweet and reminded me of something. I just couldn't put my finger on it. I ate the whole piece and asked for another. Jimmy looked at me with eyebrows raised.

"*Okay?* I guess one more won't hurt cha too bad."

Before I finished the second piece, I began to feel warmth creeping into my face. The temperature of the day seemed to be getting hotter and hotter. I started to feel a little weak in the legs, and Donald Ray kept waving back and forth. The next thing I remember was waking up in Donald Ray's old truck out in the middle of the woods. I felt a strong urge to purge my stomach. I leaned out the window and let it fly. I slumped back in the seat and gasped. Before I could relax, I had to lean out the window again. I must have passed out after that. When I finally woke up for good, I was in a sleeping bag in Bushwhacker Cave.

After I had stumbled out of the cave to relieve myself, Donald Ray filled in the missing gaps of the day. He had called Granny and told her we were going camping and that he had all the stuff I needed. He said I walked/stumbled my way to the cave. I don't remember it at all. I then passed out on the sleeping bag. I had eaten that melon at two o'clock. It was now seven thirty that night. I was starved, and my head was pounding.

"We got anything to eat?"

Donald Ray had brought a can of pork and beans and some taters. We cooked them over a fire and ate until we were stuffed. After eating, Donald Ray leaned back against the wall of the cave, looked at me, and asked, "Well, what do you think of Rube's special melons?"

"Pretty darned sweet!" I muttered. "Too sweet. They made me sick."

"It weren't the sweet that made you sick. It was the 'shine. You had way too much for your first time. It won't be so bad next time."

The way my head and body felt, I didn't think there would ever be a next time. Shine was a whole lot more potent than store-bought whiskey. Donald started recanting the entire story to me all over again. I stared at the flames of the campfire and leaned back against the rough wall of the cave. Life was so different here. I wondered what my old gang was doing tonight. They would never believe the day I had just survived. All in all, though, I was glad to be here and not there.

CHAPTER 10

Wife-Killer Boat

I had been moaning the blues to Gramps for the past month about buying a canoe or a Jon boat of my own. Gramps had a nice Jon boat he allowed me to fish from as long as he was along. I was not allowed to take it down to the creek by myself. I would be fourteen in a couple of months. I don't know why he wouldn't let me use his boat by myself. Heck far! Donald was allowed to drive, and he was a year younger than me. It just wasn't fair.

Saturday morning dawned a pink sky in the east.

"Probably going to rain by tomorrow," Granny muttered as she wiped her hands on her apron.

She was busy fixing skillet biscuits and had flour all over herself.

I stumbled out of the bedroom half awake. Between sips of coffee, Gramps watched Granny puttering around in the kitchen. I sat down to tie my boots when Gramps suddenly arose from his chair and slapped his leg with a grin on his face a mile wide.

"So you want a boat of your own, huh?"

I was wide awake and on alert. "You bet I do. Are we going to town?"

"Nope, I just had an idee. After breakfast, meet me out at the garage."

Curiosity played havoc with my appetite. I was only able to choke down three eggs, two biscuits, and a half a pound of bacon—an hors d'oeuvre compared to my usual fare.

After I helped Granny clear the table, Gramps and I headed for the garage. The garage was an old wooden two-car affair sitting by itself in the pasture out behind the house. It was built back in the thirties to accommodate Model Ts, making it too narrow for today's car sizes. Consequently, it was used exclusively for a shop on one side and Granny's storage unit on the other. Gramps had built a partition between the sides to keep Granny's stuff separate from his important tools and implements used for keeping the old farm running.

Gramps did not believe in throwing anything away. There was always the possibility that a certain piece of junk could be used for something. He had boxes of rusted bolts of every size and shape. Under his workbench resided an archaeologist's dream: rusty metal parts, empty oil cans, and rolls of wire comprised the top layer of the pile. The farther down into the pile you went, the farther back in history you were.

After my grandfather passed away, I decided to clean up his old shop. When I reached the bottom of the pile under his workbench, I found I had stepped back in time to the early 1920s. I found a calendar with a pinup Tool Mate from 1922. The exposed page was December and under the twenty-fifth; a hand-scribbled note said, "Get something for Mom." I found an envelope with gas-ration stamps from the World War I era stuffed in an antique Gulf Oil can. My most-valued treasure was an old-fashioned beer-can opener advertising for the Griesedieck (pronounced "greasy dick") Brothers beer company in St. Louis, Missouri.

Gramps rolled his acetylene welder to the front of the garage and tapped on the tanks.

"Yep, there's enough in her to do the job."

I was about to go nuts with curiosity.

"Are we going to make a boat?" I asked.

"We sure are. Go get the truck."

Hey, this was great. We were not only going to make a boat, but I was actually being asked to go get the truck. I was going to get to drive the truck the entire two hundred feet from the driveway to the garage. I couldn't wait to see what other exciting plans were in the making for me that day.

I opened the gate and jumped behind the wheel of a 1962 Chevy pickup. It was one of the kinds that had to be shifted on the steering column. Now, let's see. First gear was down and forward, second was up and forward, third was back and down, and reverse was back and up. Or was it up and forward? After a couple of jumps, hops, and killing the engine, I finally mastered the clutch and got the truck moving forward. I didn't dare try to shift on the fly, so I crept forward in first gear and made my way to the garage. I hadn't noticed that Gramps was keeping a close watch on my progress. I stopped the truck, turned off the ignition, and jumped out, proud as a game rooster.

Gramps was not about to let me know he was watching. When I looked in his direction, he was rooting around in a beat-up wooden box for his torch lighter. He seemed satisfied with what he found and headed for the truck. We drove across the field to the dump at the edge of the field.

Every farm had a dump somewhere on it. There was always a pile of charred cans from the burning barrel, worn-out window air conditioners, water heaters, and bald tires. Our dump was special. It contained an assortment of antique car-body parts because my grandfather used to do a little welding on crunched fenders for folks during the days of gas-ration stamps. Two 1942 Ford car hoods stood leaning against each other like a monolith in the middle of the dump.

Gramps made his way to the solitary piece of junkyard statuary, motioning for me to follow. He walked around the two hoods and scratched his chin in deep concentration. I stood motionless, wondering what the heck he was up to. As I stared at the two hoods, a picture began to form in my mind. No! This was not what I had in mind for a boat of my own. I looked at those rusty hoods and looked at my grandfather. My throat became very dry as I saw a smile develop on his face.

"Give me a hand."

My grandfather's voice broke the trance I was in. We loaded the two hoods in the back of the truck and drove back to the garage. Gramps set the two hoods end to end on a set of sawhorses with a couple of two-by-fours acting as a rest for the hoods to nestle into. He grabbed a brazing rod and lit his welding torch.

"Don't look at the light," he warned as he flipped his welding mask down.

I peeked through my fingers once in a while to see what progress he had made. Finally, the flame went out. Gramps flipped his welding helmet up and stepped back to admire his handiwork.

"By golly, it looks like a boat to me," he said.

You know, it really did look a little like a rusty old boat. Gramps continued to work on the boat, welding in a couple of crossbars and two seats. He used some retired license plates to cover a few of the weaker, rusted-through spots and even welded some rings on the sides and the ends. The rings in front were for tying the boat into the back of the truck, and the rings on the side were for hooking a fish stringer to.

When he was finished, he rummaged around for a can of marine-quality paint. The can said "Old Town Green." We finished painting the boat and cleaning up our work area just in time for supper. Gramps said we would launch the boat on its maiden voyage tomorrow after church.

Sunday morning bloomed with wonder and excitement. *How long is he going to preach?* I thought in frustration. I looked at my watch. He was fifteen minutes past the usual cutoff time and didn't sound like he was anywhere near done. Finally, the call for invitation. We sang the first chorus and then the second. Usually, we would then skip to the last. Not today. We had to sing all six choruses. I was out the door before the preacher could say, "Amen." Donald Ray was right behind me.

He and I were going to take my newly made boat down the Roubidoux Creek (pronounced "ruby-doo") on its maiden voyage. I was planning so many adventures in that boat I couldn't keep half of them straight. Donald Ray brought his own paddle. It was his favorite. He said it fit his hand just right. Gramps had given me a paddle to keep as my own. He had scratched my initials, MVP, with his pocketknife across the blade.

Donald Ray and I were on the way home to get that boat before Granny came out of the church. Donald Ray backed his pickup up to the boat. The sawhorses it was sitting on happened to be just the right height to slide the boat into the back of the truck. I tried pushing it into the pickup bed. It wouldn't budge. Donald Ray grabbed a side, and together we huffed and puffed that heavy son of a gun into the truck. After we tied it in, we hopped into the cab and headed for the river.

About halfway there, Donald Ray muttered, "How we gonna load that boat back into the truck when we're done?"

He was right. That thing had to weigh a thousand pounds. Actually, it was more like two hundred, but it might as well have been a thousand. I wasn't going to let that worry me and ruin my float trip. We would just deal with it when the time came.

Unloading the boat wasn't too bad. The truck was on a slope backed up to the creek. When we untied it and gave it a little shove, it unloaded itself half in the water and half on the gravel edge of the stream.

Donald Ray parked the truck, and together we pushed the boat into the water. Would it float?

Yes, it did. It floated like the beautiful boat it was. Would it float with us in it? I stepped in first. It stayed afloat. Next, Donald Ray got in. It was still floating and doing a mighty fine job of it. We were ready to head downstream.

We had arranged for Gramps to meet us in four hours at the Highway 17 bridge takeout. We had to get a move on.

I like to sit in the back and paddle and let Donald Ray keep the front end under control. We were both pretty competent paddlers since he had shown me how to do a proper "J" stroke. I started a nice, even paddle. The boat began to go in a circle. I mentioned to Donald Ray that he might help out a little. He said he was.

"This darned boat is too wide. It paddles like a washtub."

"No, it doesn't. We just need to get used to her ways."

So we made our way downstream, looking a lot like a leaf being blown about on the water in a gale. We went from one side of the creek to the other. We went through riffles backward. After about an hour we finally began to figure her out. She needed shorter strokes and twice as many.

We were able to keep her pointed in one direction most of the time. However, she still had a tendency to move from one side of the creek to the other. In spite of her weight, she had a shallow draft. We rarely had to get out and drag her through the shallows. That was fortunate. Dragging that boat through the shallows was a lot like dragging a house through the shallows.

It was a good thing the boat had a shallow draft. The sides weren't very tall, and on many occasions, we took on water over the edge, going through some tricky chutes. After four and a half hours of fierce paddling and dragging, we were relieved to see the bridge indicating the end of our journey. It was a great day. It was a long day. My boat had survived its first experience on Roubidoux Creek.

With Gramps on one end and Donald Ray and I on the other, we wrestled the boat into the truck.

"Well, boys, what do you think of the wife killer?" asked Gramps.

What in the world did he mean by that? He looked serious and then winked at Donald Ray. A wife killer was anything that needs to be moved but weighed so much you'd rather not mess with it, so you send the wife out to move it. I wouldn't wish that on anyone's wife. I would definitely get a lighter boat before I got married.

"It floated like a cork, Gramps, and didn't leak at all. The water in the bottom was from us getting in and out and from some coming over the top."

"Glad to hear it. How did she handle?"

"It took a while to get used to her, but we finally did," I said with pride.

Donald Ray muttered something about a motor or a stick of dynamite being the only solution. I knew a motor was out of the question. Gramps just acted like he didn't hear Donald Ray's comment.

The adventures we had in that boat over the next three years were unforgettable. Floating the Roubidoux by moonlight, sinking every time we turned around, floating a sick calf across the creek to its mama, and just plain serious fishing were all memories I cherished about that homemade boat.

One day we sank her in the "Twenty-Foot Hole." There was no way to retrieve her short of calling in a marine salvage company. For years after that sad day, I could peer over the edge of the swimming-hole bluff during the winter months (when the Roubidoux was at its clearest) and vaguely see the "Old Town" green paint in the shape of my boat at the bottom of the Roubidoux. As far as I know, she still sits at the bottom of the Twenty-Foot Hole directly below the steel-cable rope swing.

CHAPTER 11

Devil's Watch Goat

Few things will bring fear to the heart of a man like the growl of a big watchdog behind him. For example: the sound of a twelve-gauge pump chambering a shell in the dark when you're trespassing, the sound of your mother's footsteps when you just broke her favorite vase, or meeting a red-eyed, fire-snorting devil goat face-to-face in a narrow cave passage.

The limestone geology of the Ozark hills has fostered the formation of caves for millions of years. Caves were utilized by the Native Americans who inhabited Missouri thousands of years before white settlers ever set foot in this magical land. The caves were used by black bears before settlers extirpated them from the long list of wild animals who were Missouri's first inhabitants. In later years, Missouri's caves were used by the settlers for food storage, homes, and a myriad of other uses.

Donald Ray and I loved to explore caves along Roubidoux Creek. Listening to the old-timers, we would pick up bits of information about this cave or that one. Occasionally we would hear about a new one we didn't know about.

One Sunday in late January we overheard some old-timers talking out in front of the church about a cave on the Roubidoux we had not explored. We felt confident that we could find that cave and had to check it out that day.

We convinced Granny and Donald Ray's ma to let us go after lunch. Donald Ray came home with me. We woofed down generous helpings of roasted chicken and stuffing, mashed potatoes swimming in chicken gravy, and home-canned green beans cooked in bacon grease with fresh onions chopped up in them. A slice of Granny's boiled chocolate cake with a tall glass of ice-cold milk finished it all off.

I'm not sure why it was called "boiled" chocolate cake. It was baked in a shallow cookie-sheet-type pan and had the best chocolate fudge-style icing you ever put in your mouth. My mouth is watering just thinking about it.

We changed clothes and dressed warmly. The sky was dark and threatening snow. That wouldn't change our minds. Heck, it was warm in a cave this time of the year. That's a great thing about caves. They were at constant temperature year-round. At approximately fifty-eight degrees, they felt warm in the winter and cool on hot summer days. We set out on foot with nothing but a couple crackers and some cheese to suffice for what we liked to call survival rations.

You never knew what to expect on an adventure like this. We could get stranded in a blinding blizzard or lost in an unexplored cave that went straight to the center of the earth. We both carried a flashlight, extra batteries, and a Zippo lighter for emergencies. Donald Ray always had a little notebook in his shirt pocket. The notebook was a handy tool. We used it for passing notes in church and for starting hand-warming fires when dry kindling was hard to find. We were prepared.

We walked for about half an hour when it began to snow. The flakes were small and icy at first, but before long, they became wet and much larger. In another fifteen minutes, the ground was turning white. It looked like things might get serious. We discussed whether or not we should turn back.

After a little discussion, Donald Ray said, "Nope. We got these survival rations. Let's find that cave."

It was about four miles to where we thought the cave was. By the time we got there, the snow was up to the top of our boots. It was really coming down. The woods were totally silent except for the hiss of the falling snow.

We climbed about halfway up the side of the steep ridge running parallel to the creek and started hunting for a cave opening. Donald Ray said he thought he had heard there were actually two caves by each other. One had a large opening, and the other was pretty small. We found the small opening first.

We crawled into the cave for about three feet. The passage opened into a large room with a tall dome ceiling. The floor was covered with bowl-shaped formations filled with clear water. The room seemed magical. The reflections of our flashlights in the water-filled bowls bounced on the walls and ceilings. We sat in the cave, warming up from the winter chill outside. I played the beam of my flashlight all around the room. There was no other tunnel. This room was it.

As neat as it was to have found a cave with these unusual formations on the floor, it was disappointing that there was not more to it. Secretly, I always believed Donald Ray and I would find a secret storage of loot left behind by the James Gang in one of the caves we explored.

I decided it was time to dig into the survival rations. I was always hungry as a kid. Heck, I'm still always hungry. We munched a couple of the crackers and some of the cheese. We were careful to save some back in case we had a survival situation to deal with later.

We both took long drinks from the cold, clear water in the bowl formations. It was good. It had an earthy limestone smell, but tasted clean and refreshing.

It was time to move on. The world outside the cave had changed dramatically. We couldn't believe the amount of snow on the ground. It was shin deep and still falling hard. We really felt like early explorers now. We were facing the elements and hunting for a lost treasure. It wasn't often we had the opportunity to risk life and limb in a major snowstorm to go cave hunting, and by golly, we were going to take full advantage of it.

I led the way, and Donald Ray picked up the rear. We worked around a rock outcropping about fifty feet beyond where we had found the first cave. A narrow ledge of rock was all that was between us and a fifty-foot drop to the dark waters of the Roubidoux below.

We inched around the outcropping, and there in the corner was a cave opening big enough to walk into. The ceiling dropped ten feet in, forcing us to duck walk and finally to crawl. Donald Ray was right on my heels when we rounded a slight curve in the passage. I looked down and saw something unusual.

"What's this?"

Donald Ray mumbled that he couldn't see. I told him it looked like some white fur. There was a big glob of it on the floor. I played the beam of the flashlight farther down the passageway and saw more of it. It was all over. I started to get a creepy feeling. Something evil lived in this cave. I sensed we were in trouble.

"Donald Ray?"

"What?"

"You think we should come back with a gun?"

"Why?" he answered from behind me.

"I think there is some animal like a mountain lion or bear living in this cave."

"It's probably just a rabbit. They lose fur all the time."

"Yeah, when they're being eaten by a bear," I answered a little nervously.

I also started to smell something pretty strong on the air drafts in the passage.

"Smells like corn mash to me." Donald Ray had a noticeably higher pitch to his voice. "I think we've found old Rube's still. Keep moving, but watch out for booby traps."

As I slowly advanced down the passage, my heart leaped into my throat. Ahead of me, two red eyes looked straight at me in the pitch blackness of the cave. I stopped so fast Donald Ray ran right into me close enough to check my colon for problems.

"What the heck did you stop for?" he said in a voice a little too loud for my comfort.

"Quiet," I whispered. "There are two red eyes looking at me. It looks like the devil himself is in this cave."

I flattened myself against the side of the passage, allowing Donald Ray to peer around me. He froze. I don't know how long we sat there motionless. It might have been hours, or it might have been only seconds. The red eyes appeared to be moving toward us. My heart was racing. I tried to back up and wedged myself between Donald Ray and the wall. We were momentarily stuck. The eyes drew closer and closer. Suddenly the beam of my flashlight revealed the creature that the eyes belonged to. A large white goat stood about ten feet away.

I have never been so relieved in my life. We both started laughing. A darned goat had scared the stuffin' out of both of us. Well, we weren't going to allow a goat to keep us from our appointed task. I started forward, hollering at the goat to "get." It didn't move. I crawled to within a couple of feet, and the goat started to act like it would love nothing better than to get into a head-butting contest with me. I played my flashlight around him. He was in a large room. The narrow passage dropped off abruptly into the room. The goat was standing directly in front of the opening into the passage we were in. There was a stick tied to his middle, extending up like a single spike from the center of his back. The stick's fork was tied together under his belly and extended down about a foot. This yoke was designed to keep the goat in the room and out of the passage. Now that seemed strange to me. Why would anybody force this goat to stay in the cave?

"He's a watch goat!"

I had almost forgotten Donald Ray was behind me.

"A what?"

"A watch goat. Shiners use 'em to keep people outa their stills."

I had never heard of such a thing.

"They used to use mountain lions. Too many shiners got et up by their own watch lions, and mean-ass goats took their place."

"He doesn't seem that mean to me."

"Just try and get past 'em," Donald Ray muttered behind me.

I moved forward, talking softly to the goat.

"Nice goat. That's a good goat"

When I was about a foot from the goat, we were eye to eye. I noticed he had some big horns curled back around his head. I looked into his eyes and saw hate. He snorted, rose up on his hind legs, and lunged toward me with the firm intent to butt heads. I drew back just in time.

"Donald Ray, that darned goat nearly took my head off. When I looked into his eyes, I saw evil. They were as red as rubies and burning hot. I swear he snorted fire right before he jumped at me. Back up, man! I want outa this cave, and I want out now!"

We started scrambling backward like two crabs. The ruckus we raised got that goat all excited, and he started lunging into that passage like he was willing to die just to get one taste of our blood. His horns rang out a chilling clang each time he drove his head against the rock wall of the cave.

Donald Ray and I never went back to that cave. I had nightmares for weeks about that devil goat. Old Rube has long gone off to that whiskey still in the sky. I wonder if a ghost goat haunts that cave. I think I will go back there someday just to see...or maybe not.

CHAPTER 12

Wooden Legs Don't Float

A half mile down the road from our farm, George and Ruby Jones ran a small country store. You could pick up a gallon of milk for yourself or a salt block for the cattle. They had at least one of almost anything you would ever need.

I used to walk down to the store on Saturdays and get a sandwich and a sodie. While Ruby sliced a chunk of bologna for my sandwich, I would reach into one of those old-fashioned sodie coolers filled with chilled water and fish around for a grape Nehi. Ruby knew I liked my bologna thick and never shorted me on the amount. She would lay a piece of American cheese on it and slather on some sandwich spread. There just wasn't a better sandwich anywhere.

A gumball machine stood invitingly in a corner by the sodie cooler. Bright-orange and deep-purple orbs filled the glass barrel atop the gumball machine. Orange and grape were your only choices, making your decision easier. For a penny, you could have a piece of gum that filled your cheek like a chipmunk's pouch. Those gumballs were nearly the size of a golf ball. With a thick sandwich, a cold sodie, and a grape gumball in a brown paper sack, I was ready to go fishing.

I spent every Saturday I could fishing. I fished in old government ponds out in the national forest, neighbor's ponds, our pond, the Roubidoux Creek, and the Gasconade River. I didn't care as long as I was fishing.

This Saturday George and I were going fishing in the Roubidoux down by the old Byrd place. There was a long, deep pool known appropriately enough as the Byrd Eddy. George was a great old guy. He never had much to say, but was a good fisherman. He got around pretty well for a man with no legs. He had lost both legs years before in a deer-hunting accident and had prosthetic ones. Of course, everyone around the community referred to them as wooden legs. As far as I knew, they were wooden. I found out differently that day.

George had been hinting for a month that he wanted to try out my car-hood boat. We had arranged for me to pick him up at the store. Gramps let me use the old pickup since George was going with me. After all, I was fourteen now and could drive as well as Donald Ray. I loaded up my sack lunch and George's fishing equipment, while he hopped in the cab of the truck.

George and I unloaded the "wife killer" and slipped her into the creek. We paddled and fished down one side of the eddy and made our way back upstream on the other side. The fishing was fantastic.

George didn't fly fish. He was using some kind of a casting rod and a lure called a Rapala Minnow. The lure had two sets of treble hooks on it. I asked George if he thought six hooks were enough to catch a fish. Or was the idea to catch six fish at once? He just grinned and made no reply.

George cast his mega fish catcher up against a low bluff and started to crank it in. He hooked up almost immediately, and then something strange happened. Another fish got hooked on his lure. He had a pretty good-sized goggle-eye and a largemouth bass on at the same time. He jumped up in the boat and started laughing and making comments about fly-fishers only using one hook.

My boat was one of the most stable boats I have ever been in. The only problem it had was that its sides were low enough; it was easy to take on water.

George was working his fish and kind of lost his balance standing up in the boat. The edge dipped a little low, and my vessel started taking on water. When he realized what was happening, he stepped back and flipped over the other side of the boat. It all happened so quickly; George disappeared over the side before I could react.

I sat there for a moment, waiting for him to surface. My only thought was, *I hope those wooden legs of his float.* After a second or two passed, George did not come to the surface. I panicked and dove in after him.

I swam to the bottom, looking for him. The water was at least ten feet deep. I could see no sign of him. I surfaced for air and called out to him. Nothing! I dove again and swam, frantically looking for him in the dark water. I had to come up for air again and figured it was too late for George. If I had to come up twice, and he had not made it up, I was sure he had drowned. I called out for him one more time as soon as I hit the surface.

"Over here," he hollered.

I couldn't believe my ears; he was alive. I looked in the direction of the voice, and there stood George on the shore fishing.

"What the heck are you doing over there fishing? I nearly drowned looking for you," I said in a raised voice as panic turned to relief and then anger.

"I just walked out," he replied. "I'm not fishing. I'm still trying to land these two fish."

I swam over to my boat and pulled it to the gravel bar where George stood proudly, putting his two fish on a stringer.

"What do you mean you just walked out?"

"I mean just that. I walked out. These legs of mine sink like a rock. I just waited until I hit bottom and walked out. I kept pressure on those fish and worked 'em into the shore. I was wondering where you got off to. When I got up on shore, I didn't see you in the boat. I was so busy with my fish I didn't have time to worry about you. I knew you could swim. I figured you dropped that fly pole of yours and dove in after it."

I learned two valuable lessons that day. First, artificial legs don't float, and second, you can catch more than one fish on one of those treble hooks. That's okay. I still prefer to catch 'em one at a time on a fly I tied.

CHAPTER 13

The Day We Closed the School

Every school science fair had its share of projects from the mundane to the unusual. One year Richard Dickenson and I made a tornado with a vacuum cleaner and some steaming, hot water. It worked well, and we got a blue ribbon for our efforts.

The project I remember most fondly was the year Terry Martin and I used Terry's grandpa's original recipe for "corn squeezins." When it was time to make the mash, we each had two five-gallon glass jars filled with corn, sugar, and yeast in our lockers. We decided to time this activity so that the fermentation process took place over the weekend. Everything was set in motion on Friday during science class.

When Saturday morning came around, school was the last thing on my mind. I was headed for the Current River to do a little trout fishing with Gramps. When I climbed on the bus Monday morning, I hadn't thought about that corn mash all weekend. As the bus rolled to a stop in the gravel parking lot, everyone was staring out the windows toward the doors of the high school. The principal, the superintendent, and three janitors were directing students to the gym.

"Wonder what's going on," some kid in the back said.

Everybody was getting excited because something was definitely up. We stepped off the bus and made our way toward the school to see what was happening. The principal was motioning for us to go to the gym. We all just kept crowding toward the school to try to catch a glimpse of something.

"What's going on?"

"There is a noxious smell in the school. We're afraid it's some sort of gas leak. All of you, head to the gym pronto." The principal pointed toward the gym, and we moved in that direction.

Cool, a gas leak. No school today. Everybody was ready to celebrate. I started making plans for the rest of the day. I would be able to sneak down to the government pond I found last week and see if there were any fish in it. The old timers in the area were always putting fish in those small government ponds. You never knew what you might catch.

The little gym was filled to capacity. Students sat on the hard wooden bleachers, talking excitedly. The superintendent walked to the middle of the gym floor and held up his hands for silence. You could have heard a pen drop. He was about to say those anxiously awaited words, "Go back to your buses. There will be no school today."

Instead, he said firmly and with a great deal of agitation in his voice, "Will Mark Van Patten and Terry Martin please follow me to the high school?"

The silence in the gym was so thick you could have cut it with a knife. All eyes were on Terry and me. The smile of anticipation on our faces turned to looks of total terror. I felt the blood drain from my face in horror and then well back up in embarrassment as I made my way through the sea of bodies between me and the gym floor. As I walked across the gym floor, I could feel hundreds of eyes focused on my back.

The superintendent only called you out in front of the entire school when it was something as serious as murder. What had we done?

Terry was always a cutup and couldn't resist making a face and getting everyone to laugh as we left the gymnasium. The superintendent glared at us and very loudly explained that this was no laughing matter. We two boys had better march immediately to the high school.

As we exited the gym, we could see the principal standing with his hands on his hips fifty feet away at the front doors of the high-school building. A janitor stood on either side of him. The parking lot was still full of buses, and all the bus drivers were standing in a group, watching what was about to happen. I felt like a prisoner taking that last long walk to the gas chamber.

I was scared to death. My mind wouldn't work, and my feet felt like lead weights. The short strip of sidewalk stretched before me for miles. When we finally stopped, we stood under the vicious glare of Cleotis Tanner, our principal. He reached out, took both of us by an ear and marched us down the hall of the school.

Terry was trying to wriggle free and whimpering, "What'd we do?"

I was too scared to say a word. We stopped in front of my locker.

"Open it!" Mr. Tanner growled at me. I did what he asked.

My hands were trembling so badly it took me three times to get the combination right. The smell coming from my locker as I opened the door almost made me gag. Terry turned away, just missing Mr. Tanner's shoes as he vomited on the floor.

My eyes were burning, and the urge to gag was overwhelming. There in my locker was a bubbling mass that looked a lot like the stuff Terry had just deposited on the floor. Only the mass of putrefying liquid in my locker smelled ten times worse. There were two bloated mice floating in it!

Mr. Tanner was turning every sheet of green and trying to choke out something in the form of a question.

"Wha—wha—what is it?

"It's my science project," I whimpered between gags.

I had to slam the locker door shut to keep from throwing up all over myself.

Mr. Tanner then marched us to Terry's locker and forced him to open it. The fermenting mash in his locker was mouse free and didn't smell nearly as bad.

"I don't care if it is your science project. I want you two boys to get that stuff out of my school, and I want it out now!"

We each grabbed one of our glass jugs and left by the back door. We carried our corn mash down into a gully and poured it out. Neither of us said a word. We went back into the school and down to the science room where we washed out the jugs and put them on the shelf. Mr. Hesten, the science teacher, was standing in the door, smiling, as we turned to leave.

"I thought I told you boys to do your fermenting at home. We were only going to do the distilling here at school."

"We didn't realize how bad it would smell," I said.

"At least mine didn't have dead mice in it," said Terry.

He looked at me accusingly like this whole embarrassing affair was my fault.

"Yeah, well, it wasn't my idea to make your grandpa's moonshine either. And I couldn't take it home 'cause Granny would have skinned my hide."

"I think under the circumstances, you two should consider a different science-fair project," Mr. Hesten offered.

Fans were placed in the halls, and the janitors ran around with air freshener all day. At noon the decision to call off school early made heroes of Terry and me to the entire student body.

We decided we were going to stick with our original project and fermented our mash at Terry's grandpa's house. He was still able to give us valuable instruction in the fine art of corn-whiskey making even at the ripe old age of ninety-six.

Mr. Hesten agreed to let us do the distilling under the big ventilation hood in the science room. We produced two quarts of genuine Ozark Mountain corn squeezins. Our project, which included a paper on the chemical reactions occurring in alcohol fermentation, was awarded an honorable mention at the fair. The judges were pretty impressed with the product, but not with the presentation.

I heard later that the superintendent had told the judges not to give us anything better than an honorable mention. I also heard that one of the judges got pretty silly after sampling the product over and over just to see if it was properly done. Mr. Hesten took the remainder of the liquor home with him after allowing Terry and me one good sip apiece. Dang, that was some mighty fine squeezins!

CHAPTER 14

Rube and the Widow Bentley

Mid-July was a busy time on the farm. The hay was cut and baled. While the weather held, the bales were stacked in barns for protection until winter necessitated their presence at the feed lot.

Gramps and I were unloading a pickup load of hay bales when Rube drove up. Rube's keys had been taken away from him about a year ago by family members because his driving was a threat to the entire community. Occasionally, he would find them and head down the nearest gravel road at speeds Mario Andretti would be proud of.

Rube slid to a stop in front of the barn where Gramps and I were working. He walked into the barn, supported by one of his hand-carved walking sticks. He hobbled over to a hay bale, thumped it twice with his cane, and sat down. Gramps gave me one of those looks that said, "You keep working. I will see what's on Rube's mind."

Rube sat quietly on the hay bale, with both hands resting on the top of his ornately carved walking stick. He looked up at Gramps as he approached, turned his head, and spat a large brown, foamy glob of chewing-tobacco juice on the dirt floor of the barn.

Gramps sat down on a hay bale across from Rube. "What's on your mind, Rube?"

Rube stared at his shoes for a moment then began to speak, "George, I was reading the Bible and discovered a terrible transgression going on in this here neighborhood."

"Whaddaya mean, Rube?"

Rube cleared his throat and looked around from left to right as if he were about to reveal the mysteries of the universe. His watery, old blue eyes fixed solidly on Gramps.

"You know, George, the Bible says it is the 'sponserbility of the men folk in the community to take care of them there widers and orphans." Gramps nodded in agreement.

"It talks about seeing to their physical needs and lettin' the Lord take care of their spiritual ones."

Again, Gramps nodded. A slight grin began to spread on his face. I was getting more curious with every word Rube said. Gramps shot a glance in my direction as I tossed another bale onto the stack.

"Well, George," Rube continued, "I was thinking about the wider, Bentley."

Gramps looked contemplatively at the ground and interrupted Rube.

"She's doin' okay. Old-man Bentley left her in pretty good shape financially."

Rube gripped the top of his cane tightly, turning the knuckles of his wrinkled, old, leathery hands white.

"No, George, I believe we are supposed to take care of her physical needs. George, we ain't been doin' that. Why, that woman has been all alone since Old-man Bentley passed near a year ago."

Gramps had seen this coming from a mile away. He knew old Rube too well.

"Rube, I'm going to have to leave that up to you. I'm just too darned old."

Gramps was pushing a young seventy-two years of age. Rube was waving goodbye to ninety.

He looked straight into Gramp's eyes and said firmly, "Well, I ain't. I can take care of the 'sponserbility the Lord put on us."

I buried my head in the stack of hay, trying to stifle my laughter. Gramps just grinned, stood up, and bid Rube farewell.

Sunday morning the menfolk stood in a semicircle in front of the church door, talking before services began. Rube drove up and hurried over in his distinctive, shuffling gait. He was looking down at the ground and wearing the funniest-looking oversized sunglasses I had ever seen. Nothing surprised me about Rube. He constantly came up with outlandish getups.

As we started to drift into the church for the beginning of the services, Rube was forced to remove his sunglasses. His right eye was all puffed up and just as black as any black eye I had ever seen.

"What happened to your eye, Rube?" my grandfather asked with a slight grin on his face.

"I would just as soon not talk about it, George," Rube said while staring at the floor.

"Did the widow, Bentley, do that to you?"

Gramps was about to burst out laughing.

Rube hesitated for a moment and muttered, "I was just trying to do the right thing by her."

Gramps and I had to leave the church. I couldn't remember laughing so hard before or since.

Granny found us out in the truck waiting when services were over. Gramps and I told her the story through tears of laughter and guffaws. Granny wasn't pleased about us missing church and found no humor in the story at all.

All she could say was, "Poor Mrs. Bentley. I better go check up on her this afternoon. You boys better get me home. I need to bake her a pie. Poor Mrs. Bentley."

Granny's cure for all that ailed you was a fresh-baked pie.

CHAPTER 15

How Big Was That Bomb?

Living just a short distance as the crow flies from a military installation could lead to some exciting opportunities. This was especially true for a couple of adventurous boys like Donald Ray and me. Occasionally, the military would stage war games out in the national forest. The Mark Twain National Forest made up a large portion of the county we lived in. Since it was federally owned, it was appropriate for the Army to use the land for military training. That suited Donald Ray and me completely.

When rumors of suspicious movement in the forest made it to one of us, we were on the road, looking for action. The soldiers would incorporate us into their maneuvers. We were the official countryside peasants acting as "friendly locals to the troops." We would drive them around in our old pickup we named Roscoe, since that was the name of the previous owner (almost everything had a name. I even had a screwdriver named Floyd), sneak in a little "shine" to the officers and sometimes actually partake in a real mission. One time we were taught how to take fingerprints.

Our mission was to drive over to Donald Ray's uncle's farm and look for a guy hanging out in the barn. He was supposed to be one of ours (the good guys). He was a downed pilot behind enemy lines. We were to take his fingerprints, drop them off at a later-disclosed location, and wait for further instructions. We were then told the pilot was actually one of ours and not an enemy spy trying to find our headquarters. It was our job to go pick him up and safely transport him to HQ for a debriefing.

On this particular mission, we were ambushed, and our pilot was taken captive. Donald Ray and I were scared silly when that bunch of screaming bad guys jumped out of the trees all around us. We were only too happy to let them take the prisoner. However, they also took us. They questioned us for hours about the location of the good-guy's camp. We never gave in to them. After all, the future of democracy was in our hands.

After a few weeks of playing army, the soldiers would pack up and disappear without a word. They always left behind a pile of toys for us as a thank-you for our help. What we called toys included coils of underwater fuse, fuse igniters, simulator hand grenades, and other assorted items of fascination for fourteen- to fifteen-year-old boys to play with.

On one of the missions we participated in, we learned how to mix diesel fuel and ammonium-nitrate fertilizer to make a bomb. Donald Ray and I were very curious about this explosive mixture and decided we should give it a try. We rattled around the shop and found some ammonium-nitrate fertilizer in twenty-five and one-hundred-pound bags. I started to drag a one-hundred-pound bag to the truck when Donald Ray stopped me.

"I think Pa'll miss a hundred pounds of fertilizer. Maybe we should just take one of them twenty-five pounders."

I agreed wholeheartedly. That one-hundred-pound bag was just too darned heavy to mess with.

We worked up the recipe just like the soldiers had explained. Donald Ray came up with a blasting cap his uncle had left over from blasting some stumps out of a newly cleared pasture. We had fifty feet of fuse and an igniter. We were in business. Neither of us actually thought the bomb would work, but it was fun imagining that it would.

"Maybe we could blow that old stump out in the field down on the Jones place," Donald Ray speculated.

That stump had been a thorn in our side for years. It was just short enough that the grass would hide it in the spring before haying season. We would take the tractor down to the Roubidoux to do some fishing and smack into it. The last time that happened I took a nasty gash in the shin. I had a personal grudge against that darned stump.

"That's the best idea you've had in years. I would love to see that stump blown to smithereens."

We took our twenty-five-pound bag of fertilizer, blasting cap, and fuse, loaded up Old Roscoe, and drove the four miles to the Jones place. It was mid-August, hot and, as is always the case in Missouri, very humid. The hay had been cut for weeks, so the stump was easily spotted. I was a little concerned about the dry condition of the grass and wondered about fire getting out.

"I think it's mostly just a loud bang and concussion," Donald Ray assured me.

We scouted the area for a place to duck behind and watch the explosion. An ancient elm tree, consumed by Dutch elm disease, laid prostrate at the edge of the pasture. I figured it was about one hundred feet from the blast site. We could safely hide behind its huge mass.

Donald Ray went right to work, digging a shallow hole, setting the bag of fertilizer in the hole next to the stump, and pushing the blasting cap down into the mixture. I attached the fuse igniter to the other end of the fifty feet of fuse. When Donald Ray was finished, he walked over to where I laid in wait to light the fuse.

"How long does it take for this fuse to burn?' I asked.

"Dunno," Donald Ray mumbled. "I reckon that we should run like the wind as soon as we light her."

I nodded in agreement and pulled the ring on the igniter. The plastic coating on the fuse began melting as it worked its way toward the bomb.

I dropped the igniter, and we both ran full tilt toward the fallen elm. We leaped over the thick trunk and dived to the ground behind our safety bunker. We laid there, holding our ears for an eternity.

Finally, Donald Ray said, "I think it's a dud."

I peered over the top and saw that the fuse was still burning and had at least three feet left to go. Donald Ray started to look over the top of the trunk too.

I grabbed his arm and yelled, "It's about to blow!"

We started to laugh because neither of us thought it would do anything except the blasting cap might blow some of the contents out of the bag.

Before we could cover our ears, the ground shook violently, followed by the loudest noise I had ever heard. The huge old elm tree actually tried to roll over on us. Everything seemed to happen in slow motion. About the time I thought it was over, dirt, rocks, and all kinds of debris began to drop on us. More and more debris fell. We were literally buried in a pile of dirt and rock.

I clawed my way out from under the pile in time to see Donald Ray poke his head up through the dirt. He had a nasty gash over his left eye. I had a ringing in my ears so loud I couldn't hear Donald Ray's voice. His mouth was moving so I knew he was trying to say something. He motioned that his ears were ringing as well. At exactly the same time we both realized that our bomb had worked and wondered if the stump had survived the blast. Since we could not hear each other, communication was strictly on a hand-gesture basis.

We stood up and stared in amazement at the destruction that laid before us. The stump was gone and so was the earth below it for four feet and all the earth around it for ten feet in diameter. A huge, gaping hole had replaced the stump.

My mind snapped back to the scene in the shop earlier that week: "I think Pa will miss a hundred pounds of fertilizer. Maybe we should take one of them twenty-five pounders." If that conversation had not taken place, there would have been a crater to rival the Grand Canyon where Donald Ray and I had been hiding from the blast.

Granny always said that Donald Ray and I had a guardian angel watching over us every second of every day. I don't believe I would have been here to tell this story if it wasn't so. I hate to think about all that we put that poor angel through.

CHAPTER 16

The Roubidoux
(Pronounced *Ruby-doo*)

The Roubidoux Creek runs through my soul
On her long voyage to the sea.
Her life-giving water courses through my veins.
She's part of the whole that makes me.
—*Mark Van Patten*

It is a known scientific fact that, when you mix water with boys, you get magic. Donald Ray and I had many adventures and misadventures on Roubidoux Creek. Float trips in the blackest of nights, old outboard motors that never worked when you really needed them, gigging (spearing fish) when the ice froze to your gig handle, and huge midnight fires to thaw your frozen bodies from those same gigging trips are all stories worthy of mention. I think these are some of the most memorable.

*****

Scalpel, Forceps, Sponge!

I tried for years to convert Donald Ray to fly-fishing. He did purchase a fly rod. I believe I saw him use it once for about ten minutes. I think it finally found a use as a switch for moving the calves across the road, but never was used to catch a fish. One of my most memorable fishing trips with Donald Ray was also the most painful of fishing trips for him.

Usually, when Donald Ray and I decided to go fishing, it was either the night before or that very moment. I think we must have decided Saturday night to skip church for this particular trip. The big man upstairs might have decided we needed a little lesson in why you should not skip church to go fishing. We would never forget this whippin'.

The sky was the color of orange sherbet in a light-blue glass bowl. The occasional puff of white from a small cumulus cloud dotted the sky like miniature marshmallows.

I love the smell of the Ozarks early on a summer morning. I could smell hay fresh cut yesterday, lying in wait for the sun to dry it for baling. The Roubidoux had a smell of its own. I called it, "that late-summer, low-water smell." It was earthy, wet, and inviting.

Donald Ray had brought his johnboat for this trip. It was a pretty cool boat. I mean it was cool, literally. Donald Ray was always thinking. He had decided that the original color of dark olive absorbed the heat and made mid-day fishing a bit more uncomfortable. So he painted his boat bright yellow. He would have used white but didn't want to scare off all the fish. Everybody knows that fish are spooked by bright colors, especially white. I was never really sure what the reasoning behind bright-banana-yellow was. Nevertheless, we launched the small craft on a trip that would rival that of the SS Minnow and its historic three-hour cruise.

I sat in the front with my fly rod, and Donald Ray paddled and ran the trolling motor, as was the custom. Whoever's boat we used had to do all the motoring, and the other got to kick back and fish. The one in the back did get to fish the slower-moving eddies, and this was where Donald Ray got into his trick bag.

We had gone down the shady side of the Thomas Eddy and started down the opposite side when Donald Ray decided to cast to a likely looking spot near some downed trees. He flipped the bale on his open-face, spinning reel and let loose a cast with a Rapala Minnow dangling from the end of his line. The lure was a floating one with three sets of treble hooks along the bottom.

Donald Ray gave the lure a jerk, causing it to sink under the water and slip to the left like a wounded minnow. It then floated to the surface. It was a very enticing-looking meal for a big, old, hungry bass.

With the second jerk, the lure went under again and slipped to the right. It didn't float back up. Donald Ray pulled up on the rod to set the hook and realized immediately he was hung up on something under water. He pulled, jerked, and yanked, trying to break it loose from whatever held it tight. On the third yank, he was successful. The lure came free and flew through the air like a missile.

The lure stopped with a smack against Donald Ray's leg. I thought, *I'm glad that thing is loose. Now we can get on with our fishing without having to paddle over there, scaring off the fish.*

I noticed Donald Ray was just sitting there, looking at his leg. He was not making any move to cast again. I glanced at his leg and bile rose in my throat. All three sets of treble hooks were planted firmly in the calf of his leg.

Neither of us had ever dealt with that many hooks before. We had both removed a single hook from a finger or ear by pushing it through and cutting off the barb. This number of hooks presented some major problems.

First, we could not push all the hooks through. The treble hooks would not allow it. Donald Ray would not let me cut off the hooks from the lure. He paid too much for it to just ruin it. Finally, Donald Ray decided I would have to cut them out with a fillet knife. I can still feel the fear in my hands as I write about it. It is like that feeling that runs up your toes when you are standing too close to the edge of a very high cliff.

Donald Ray was pretty darned tough for a guy that didn't weigh ninety pounds soaking wet. He grimaced and cursed under his breath. When I was finally done filleting his leg like a bluegill, he was ready to get back to fishing. The bottom of Donald Ray's boat was no longer banana yellow. He had bled profusely while I was cutting out the hooks. The bleeding stopped as he tied a bandana around his leg for a bandage. Later that evening he rubbed in some Watkins bag balm, used for irritated milk-cow teats, and called it good. As a plastic surgeon, I wasn't too bad. There were only three very small scars to tell the tale.

I believe that was the last time for many years that we skipped church to go fishing.

*****

Stop, Thief, or I'll Shoot Yer Ass!

Friday evening, after the chores were finished, I started packing for the road. Donald Ray and I were headed for the Roubidoux at seven o'clock tonight. We were going to sleep under the stars and get up early to fish. Donald Ray and I were always heading out to sleep under the stars.

We had our routine. I would bring some potatoes, pork and beans, and ketchup. Donald Ray would bring hamburger, Velveeta cheese, and cooking grease. We had a permanent stash of salt and sodas in a shack on the old "Dolly" place. When we left home to rough it in the wild, we called it "Goin' John Wayne'n."

We were going John Wayne'n down by the Thomas Eddy where Prairie Creek emptied into the Roubidoux. There were only two ways to get there. Either you floated the Roubidoux for miles, or you drove through land owned by Donald Ray's family. There wasn't really any road. You just had to know where to drive through the woods and fields to get there.

It was our favorite place to camp. In all the years we camped there, I only remember seeing another soul one time. That is another entirely different story. I may or may not get around to telling that one.

After setting up camp, which consisted of collecting firewood and rolling out the sleeping bags, we decided to fix our favorite camp food. We called it gigging stew. It was nothing at all like stew. But it was darned good. We would brown a pound of hamburger and then drain off the grease to fry potatoes in later. We would then add a big can of pork 'n' beans, a block of Velveeta cheese, and half a bottle of ketchup to it. We would heat it until the cheese melted and chow down right out of the pan. Less mess to clean up that way. It was best to let Donald Ray eat first. He was a little guy and ate less than me. When he had his fill, I would eat what was left. Usually, that was way over half. It's no wonder I got to be as big as I am. We ate well, and we ate plenty. Speaking of eating, this story includes a chance meal of watermelon provided by his majesty, the king of watermelons, Rube.

Rube's watermelon patch was on the Roubidoux bottoms. Like our campsite, there were only two ways to get there. You either drove through Rube's place, or you floated down the Roubidoux. If your intention was to steal a melon, you didn't want to drive through his place. Actually, there was no real reason to steal a melon from Rube. If you asked for one, he would give it to you. It's just that a stolen watermelon tasted sweeter than a freely given one. I'm sure you already know that. Everyone knows that.

Rube was an avid hunter. As far as I knew, he only hunted one animal. That animal was the wild-eyed, slouched-shouldered melon thief. He preferred to scare the bejeezus out of the crafty critters instead of actually catching them.

The wily weasels only struck on the darkest of nights. A moon would shine on their antics, and Rube would have them before they set foot in his patch. On those nights when the moon was nowhere to be seen, and the coal, dark sky had only the Milky Way to break the monotony of its blackness, the creature would do its best to beat old Rube out of a ripe melon. The sneaky rascals were pretty good at picking a nice, ripe melon with no more than a thump on its side. On this particular night, the wild-eyed creature was yours truly.

Donald Ray held the boat in a fast chute, ready for a quick getaway. I eased over the side onto the soft sand and picked my way to the melon patch. I knew exactly where I was going. Earlier that evening, I had spied the melon I was after as we floated by in pursuit of fish.

This melon spoke to me. It was huge and just the right color. I knew from my years of experience that it would be a great melon. I reached the spot where I knew it to be. I groped in the darkness for its smooth skin. My hand brushed it, and a jolt of excitement rushed up my spine.

I quickly broke the vine loose and tucked the melon under my arm. I made my way silently to the waiting boat. Two yards from the boat, the silence of the night was split by the strong demanding voice of Rube.

"Stop, thief, or I'll shoot yer ass!"

I knew there was only one way to save my life. I threw the melon into the boat, diving headfirst into it as Donald Ray began to paddle madly downstream. Before you could say, "Jack Robinson," there were two explosions from a double-barreled twelve-gauge shotgun. Rube always fired into the air. He didn't actually want to hit anybody. He just wanted to have a good laugh. And that was exactly what he did.

We were humiliated by the sound of Rube's laughter for half a mile downstream. To add insult to injury, the melon had exploded when it hit the bottom of the boat. The contents of its belly were scattered all over the boat. Not much was left for actual eating. Oh well. The excitement was worth the effort.

We continued to play this game with Rube for many years to come. As a side note: I never succeeded in stealing one of Rube's melons without getting caught. I think Rube had some kind of ESP or something. He always knew when we would be there.

*****

Pa Is Gonna Kill Us!

The summer of '68 was as hot as any in Missouri. Humidity was so high even the fish were sweaty. Donald Ray and I worked in the hay that summer until all the hay was in. We always ended up brown as chocolate cake from the waist up. You just didn't wear shorts in the hayfield. One good rake across the thigh by a blackberry briar would press that message home in a hurry.

After weeks of stifling barn lofts, heat headaches, arms scratched raw by briars and sharp stubble, and angry red wasps, Donald Ray and I decided it was high time for a little John Wayne'n on the Roubidoux. I told Granny and Gramps, Donald Ray told Ma and Pa, and we headed out. It was customary for Donald Ray and me to take a two-week vacation after haying season was over. So our folks were not concerned. They knew roughly where we were and knew we could take care of ourselves. If we got into trouble, it wasn't more than a couple of miles to a house and a phone.

We had packed enough salt, lard, coffee, and emergency rations of dried beans and Coffee-Mate to last for the entire two weeks. You see, we lived off what Mother Earth would provide for our daily meals. We usually harvested plenty of fish, squirrels, and frog legs to do just fine.

We always brought a .22 rifle and a couple of hunting knives to gather food. I had my fly rod and a handful of popping bugs. Donald Ray brought his spinning rod, a small box of beetle spinners, and his famous goggle-eye spoon. He would solder a hook down the inside of a silver-colored fishing spoon–type spinner. He then impaled a short piece of red plastic worm on the hook as a trailer and fished it very slowly in deep water. He could catch more goggle eye than anyone I ever knew on that crazy-looking lure.

We arrived at our customary camping spot at the junction of Prairie Creek and the Roubidoux and set up camp on the gravel bar. I grabbed my fly rod and headed for the creek. Donald Ray had a hankering for squirrel, so he slipped into the woods with the .22.

I fished for an hour with nothing to show for it. The fish just were not cooperating at all. I had only brought top-water poppers, and the fish were staying deep. The water in the Roubidoux was bathtub warm. Oxygen levels had to be at the bottom of the well. I caught one small bass on the way back to camp. It was so small I could have swallowed it whole if a game warden showed up.

I knew that was not much of a concern. I had not seen a game warden on that part of the creek in my entire life. It just wasn't possible without bushwhacking for a couple of miles from the nearest road. I decided to keep it so I could at least have something to eat.

Donald Ray came back to camp shortly after I arrived.

"Them there squirrels ain't moving a stitch. I ain't heard nary a sound the whole time I was in them there woods. Just too darned hot for 'em."

I showed Donald Ray the puny fish I had. I cut off the fillets and had two one-inch-square pieces of fish flesh. We decided to start a camp stew. It was beginning to look like food might be scarce.

A camp stew was one that you built on. Each day you add to it whatever you could catch. That night we boiled some water and added the fish, some salt, and a couple teaspoons of powdered Coffee-Mate. We thought the white color from the Coffee-Mate would make it look like chowder. Keeping with the chowder theme, we cut up a potato into small, bite-sized pieces to assist our pitiful stew in appearing more nourishing. We sipped some of the soup, ate a couple pieces of potato, and decided to go hungry for the night. We would add more to the stew tomorrow.

I got up right before daylight and made coffee. I wanted to get into the creek before the sun could warm it. We needed fish for breakfast.

My stomach was doing a rendition of the *1812 Overture*. There was no question—I needed food.

After a quick cup of coffee to clear out the cobwebs accumulated by sleeping on a gravel bar, I waded into the night-cooled waters of the Roubidoux. I began false casting to get some line out. My first cast dropped the popper perfectly under an overhanging branch. Something should have nailed it the moment it hit the water. The ripples from the fly hitting the water dissipated. Still nothing. I stripped the line, causing the popper to produce that customary "blurp" in the water. Still nothing.

I fished with no success for about thirty minutes. I was so hungry the camp stew began to sound good. My mind had blocked out the foul taste it had last night. I imagined clam chowder and waded quickly to shore and breakfast.

When I got back to camp, Donald Ray was sitting up with his sleeping bag draped over his shoulders, sipping on a cup of coffee. He looked deep in thought.

"What's up, man?" I asked.

He only grunted. I let him be and dipped out some stew. It wasn't much better, but the fish flavor was a little more dominant.

We sat there in silence for a long while. Donald Ray would get in these solemn moods sometimes. The best thing to do was to leave him alone.

One thing you need to know about Donald Ray. He might talk country and dress like an old hillbilly farmer, but he was a highly intelligent, thinking man. In high school he was always on the honor roll, and he did very well in college. When he was in one of his moods, he was probably designing a better hydraulic system for his hay lift. You just never knew where his mind was or what he was thinking. Like most hill folk, he was private with his thoughts. If you bothered him when he was thinking, he would mumble angrily, and you got the message to leave him alone.

A few feet from where we sat commiserating, a cardinal began a loud rendering of its favorite notes. It went on and on. I finally had enough of its loud mouth and mumbled something about breaking its beak. The bird just ignored me and kept on singing.

I picked up a good-sized rock from the gravel and sidearmed it in the general direction of the bird to scare it off. Instead, its musical concert was interrupted by an abrupt squawk and then silence.

Donald Ray and I both turned our heads in the direction of the bird. There it laid on the ground, deader than a door nail. I couldn't believe it. I could not have hit that bird in a million years if I had tried. Well, I wasn't going to let it go to waste. I plucked it and added its breast to the stew. Donald Ray never said a word, but I could tell he was not really happy about the dead bird in the stew.

I decided to try a little bait fishing in a deep hole downstream a ways. I had a popping bug that was falling apart. I cut the body from the hook and then tied the bare hook on my leader. I took some of the bird entrails and headed downstream. I knew that my place in heaven had been sacrificed already when I decided to cook a cardinal, so bait fishing would just be one more deadbolt on that door.

I fished for an hour without a bite when suddenly I felt a tug on the line. I set the hook and felt dead weight. I brought the heavy object to the surface and at first thought I had hooked a rock. Upon closer examination, I realized it was a freshwater mussel. I kept the mussel with the intent that it would add the "clam" to the clam chowder I kept thinking I could turn our stew into. No fish would consider eating redbird entrails, so I gave up on trying to catch a fish with a hook.

I was getting desperate. I had decided to try to spear a fish and hunted for a straight and strong stick along the creek bank. I was lucky and found a great stick. A beaver had known I would be needing such a stick and obliged me. He chewed it off to just the right length and peeled all the bark off for me. I lashed my hunting knife to one end of the stick and made a great-looking spear. Now all I had to do was stand still long enough for a fish to swim by, and supper would be served.

A large hog molly sucker was only a couple of feet out of my reach and working my way when I noticed the sound of an airplane. Actually, my subconscious had registered the sound quite a bit earlier. But now my conscious mind was realizing that the plane had been directly overhead for quite some time. I glanced up and saw a conservation airplane circling overhead like a big white-and-green vulture. Instinctively, I crouched down as if to hide myself against the dark waters of the Roubidoux.

I began to think about what that guy in the plane was seeing. Here was some browned-by-the-sun wild boy, stark naked except for a belt and knife sheath, crouching down against the water in such a manner as to allow his snow-white fanny to shine like the proverbial diamond in a goat's butt. At this realization, I let out a horrified war whoop and ran toward the woods to escape the gawking of the occupants of that plane. Can you imagine the story the pilot had to tell at the end of that day?

I could tell it was late morning by the position of the sun as I entered camp. Donald Ray was nowhere in sight. I used my knife to force open the mussel. It all looked pretty gross to me. But I cut out what I figured was for eating and washed it off in the stream. I stirred it into the pot and gave the bubbling brew a sniff. It was getting pretty thick, so I added more water to it. We kept the stew cooking slowly day and night over the perpetual campfire.

The stew was beginning to smell passable to me. I was starving. I found a cup and dipped some up. I sat down and prepared to eat a late breakfast or early lunch, whichever suited your fancy. I took a spoonful of stew and blew on it until I figured it was cool enough to eat. My first thought was, *Not bad!*

After a second or two my brain registered just how bad this concoction really was. I nearly threw up. At that moment I heard a single shot ring out just over the ridge. The .22 was gone, so I assumed Donald Ray had bagged a squirrel.

Thank goodness. This stew was really bad. I dumped it out, washed out the pan, and prepared to cook up some squirrel. I could taste it now. Sure hope it was a young one. I heard Donald Ray thrashing around in the brush, heading for camp. He was grunting like he was dragging something pretty darned big. By the noise he was making, it must be "Squirrelzilla."

Donald Ray finally huffed and puffed his way into camp. There at his feet was a young black angus calf. I nearly choked.

"Pa is gonna kill us!" I whined.

"No, he won't, if he don't know," Donald Ray warned.

After the initial shock, my brain began to imagine hamburger, steak, and ribs. Since we didn't exactly have a butcher shop there on the gravel bar, new and unrecognizable cuts would be at the top of the menu. Roubidoux strip veal was my favorite.

We set to work preparing the meat to last a while. We cut must of it up into long, thin strips and salted it down. We then hung them in the sun to dry into jerky. The ninety-plus-degree temps helped take care of that for us. We cut out the tenderloin and cooked it up for lunch, with leftovers for supper. We truly feasted.

Two days later I was puttering around camp when I noticed something strange. The ants had been attracted to where I poured out the camp stew. All the ants were dead. I'd say that was not a good sign.

Donald Ray had probably saved our lives the day he killed that calf. Pa never knew about this, or it would have been our last supper.

CHAPTER 17

Lipstick, Trout, and Apple Juice

Gramps and I were up until after the news Friday night. We were tying flies, cleaning fly lines, and soaking leaders. I had to reorganize my fly boxes every time we prepared for a fishing trip. Somehow Gramps kept his fly boxes perfectly organized between trips. All his dry flies were perfectly aligned in neat little rows. He didn't spend much time on nymphs or streamers. Gramps had a simple philosophy about fly-fishing. If it couldn't be caught on a dry fly, it wasn't worth catching. Although he was pretty fond of an olive marabou leech for those really tough days.

I liked fishing a good insect hatch with a dry fly as well as anybody. But I learned early that more fish were caught below the surface than on top. Gramps accused Granny and me of bait fishing on more than one occasion when we were using subsurface flies.

One instance I recall as particularly humorous is when Gramps caught Granny putting lipstick on a wool grub she liked to fish with. She would put a small red dot on the end of the grub to represent the head. Granny was catching one fish after another, and Gramps had pretty well been skunked up to that point. He waded over close enough to her to get a peek at what she was fishing with. He wouldn't want her to know he was looking, so he acted as if he was tying on another fly. When Granny pulled out the lipstick and painted the end of a freshly tied on wool grub, he nearly fell in.

Gramps gasped out loud and sputtered, "Granny! What in the world are you doing? Don't you know it's against the law to be bait fishin' in this here fly water?"

"I'm not bait fishin'. Mind your own business, old man!" Granny turned her back to him and finished doctoring up her fly.

"If I see a game warden, you'll be thinking none of my business." Gramps stomped off downstream, fuming mad.

Roger Talbert had been the conservation agent at Montauk State Park for fifteen years. He knew all the locals and most of the out-of-town regulars by their first names. Roger was standing behind a large sycamore tree about twenty feet from where my grandparents had just had their argument. He knew my grandmother had been putting lipstick on her flies and didn't really have any problem with that. He didn't know of any regulations that prohibited it, so it was completely legal in his mind.

Things are pretty slow today, Roger thought to himself. *I think I'll have a little fun at George's expense.*

He had noticed Gramps was eating an apple while he was fishing. Roger stepped out from behind the tree and caught Granny's attention. He held a finger up to his lips, motioning for Granny to be quiet about his presence.

He slipped in behind Gramps without a sound. Gramps was concentrating intently while he tied on a new fly. He still had the apple. He had wedged it between his waders and his chest to hold it in place while he tied on his fly.

Roger waited patiently as Gramps finished and made a cast. The #16 Renegade dry fly landed delicately on the water, and immediately a hungry trout engulfed it. Gramps fought the fish for a couple of minutes before landing it with his net. He took the fly from the trout's lip and started to put it on his stringer.

"Nice fish, George," Roger said as he stepped into Gramps's line of vision.

Gramps jumped a little, startled by the voice announcing a presence from out of nowhere. He saw who it was and relaxed. He had known Roger since his first day on the job fresh out of the academy.

Roger gave Gramps a stern look and told him to step out of the water in a very law-enforcing tone of voice. Roger had raised his voice just enough that Granny and a couple other old timers in the near vicinity heard it. Gramps had a look of horror mixed with total confusion on his face. He finished stringing the fish and stepped out of the water and faced the agent.

"George, I thought you knew better than to bait fish in this here fly water. In fact, George, I thought bait fishing was against your personal philosophy. I could not believe what I just witnessed. George Van Patten was using bait on his fly."

Gramps's mouth open and closed like a fish out of water. Nothing came out.

"Well, George, what do you have to say for yourself?"

Gramps could not believe what he was being accused of. The color in his face deepened to a crimson red. He was getting mad, not scared. It was a crime against heaven in Gramps's mind to use bait to catch a trout.

"Roger Talbert! I cannot believe you could stand there and accuse me of committin' such a sin! I would just as soon have my own hand cut off before I would use bait on one of my flies."

"Well, you better start cuttin', George. I watched you covertly rub apple juice on your fly."

Gramps stuttered and stammered. He knew he had not done what he was accused of. He also knew there was no way on God's green earth he could prove it because he was eating an apple while he had tied on his fly.

Roger saw that he had Gramps right where he wanted him when Gramps's shoulders dropped in submission.

"Roger, you have known me for all these years, and you have never known of me using bait. I admit I was eatin' this here apple while I was fishing. But I never thought about the juice getting on my fly. I suppose you have to do what you have to." Gramps held out his hands to be handcuffed.

"George, I'm not going to arrest you." Roger glanced in Granny's direction to make sure she was listening. "If you had been doing something legal like putting lipstick on your fly, I wouldn't have thought a thing about it." Roger couldn't hold back a smile. Gramps looked right into Rogers eyes and knew he had been tricked.

"Roger, you ornery son of a bitch. You sure had me going. You mean to tell me it's legal for Mildred to use that lipstick?"

"It is as far as I know, George. I'm not too sure about apple juice though," Roger said with a big, toothy grin. "Go on and catch some more fish. Leave Mildred alone. Life'll go a lot easier on you if you do," Roger said as he disappeared behind another tree.

CHAPTER 18

Woodstock

They say three hundred thousand people showed up for the most famous rock concert in history. Nearly a million say they were there. Go figure. I will tell you a story about the time Donald Ray and I went to Woodstock. You decide if we were there or not.

Donald Ray and I used to tag along with Pa when he would take an old cow to the stockyard in Springfield. Pa would drop us off along Sunshine and Glenstone and then head over to the stock-yards. I was a full fifteen years of age, and Donald was sneaking up on fourteen.

One particular trip to Springfield marked our place in history. We were walking along Sunshine, headed for Leong's What-A-Burger when we decided to take a quick run through the local head shop. That is what they called the stores that sold everything from incense and candles to smoking papers and pipes. We liked to check out the albums, 8-tracks, and cool-looking stuff in the glass display cases.

A good-looking gal in tight, bell-bottom blue jeans and a halter top caught my eye immediately after walking into the store. I elbowed Donald Ray and nodded in her direction. He was already zeroed in. Being country boys, we were not exactly tutored in the proper way to approach a good-looking babe. So we just looked at the floor and kept moving. I couldn't help myself though. I sneaked more than one look at her every time I thought she wasn't likely to see me. She had on a headband of red, white, and blue beads that formed a peace sign in the middle of her forehead. Her tight bell-bottoms were frayed perfectly along the bottoms, exposing her delicate, sandaled feet. As my eyes rose from admiring her feet, I felt a hot rush flow through my face, realizing she was watching me. She smiled as if to say, "*Hi, come on over.*" So I did.

"Hi, far-out headband," was all I could muster.

"You going to the concert?" A sultry voice that made my boyhood layers melt away to expose a man ready to conquer the world came from her mouth. I stood at least a foot taller.

"Uh-huh. Uh, what concert?"

"Woodstock! You know, the most far-out coolest concert in the world."

I was not about to admit I had no idea what she was talking about.

"Uh, yeah. We are. My buddy, Donald Ray, and I have been planning it for months."

"So you are here to pick up your tickets too?"

She had a seductive sparkle in her eye that would not allow this fifteen-year-old, hormone-controlled boy to say anything but, "Yep. That's why we're here. Where are they selling them tickets anyway?"

"Right over at that counter." She pointed in the direction of a counter where Donald Ray was reading a poster about the concert.

"Oh, I see my buddy is already over there getting his ticket. I guess I better get over there. See you around maybe." I was really trying to act cool.

"See you there. Peace, and remember love is free," she said as my heart did four flip-flops.

I made my way to the counter and whispered to Donald Ray that we had to buy tickets to that woodchuck or woodstick or wood-something concert, and we had to do it now. I was about to hook up with the girl of my dreams.

There was an unwritten rule among male adolescents. No matter what, you never bust a guy's cool. Donald nodded, and we proceeded to spend all our lunch and spending money for two tickets to some concert. After we left the head shop, we took a look at our tickets and realized to our total disappointment that the concert was in New York!

After the initial frustration of realizing we could not go to New York for this concert, and I would not have the opportunity to get to know that total cutie, I began to complain about not getting to go.

"What do you mean we can't?"

He immediately started planning. That was the way Donald Ray always thought. If you told him he couldn't do something, he would make it happen. The first thing we had to do was get a better set of wheels than Old Roscoe. For that, we would need some cash. There was an aged sawmill built by his grandpa on Donald Ray's family farm. It still worked, so we decided to do some logging and milling.

I have never worked so hard in my life. We cut down trees with a trunk diameter of twenty to twenty-five inches. That's a big tree by anyone's standards. Some of the logs were eighteen to twenty feet long. I probably don't need to mention that those logs weighed in the tons.

Donald Ray had all the equipment necessary for us to go into the lumber-making business. He had an old Farmall M with lift arms and log hooks, cant hooks, a sawmill with a carriage run by the rear axle of a 1959 Chevy pickup, and the motivation to do the job. With a little practice and some good advice from Pa, Donald Ray was able to master the sawing of a log in the most efficient way to produce the most lumber from it.

My job was to roll the logs up onto the carriage, twist them into position for cutting, and finally to "off bear" and stack. The off bearing was traditionally reserved for the special person that was strong on brawn and weak on brains. All the off bearer did was grab the slabs and lumber as they came off the saw and stack them in the appropriate piles.

This might not sound too difficult. Don't be too quick to judge until you have grabbed an eighteen-foot toothpick with a four-hundred-pound chunk of wood on the other end and then try to get it off the saw before it twists and the saw blade kicks it hard enough to knock you to the ground.

When we filled the back of a pickup with lumber, we hauled it to a local post-treating and lumber plant for sale. We got pretty good change for our lumber. Donald Ray believed a two by four should be two inches by four inches. He refused to use the accepted 1 3/4 inch by 3 3/4 inch for a two by four. The old-timers who frequented the plant we sold to appreciated our lumber for that reason.

We saved up and finally had the money to buy a car. Red Southard had a 1962 Plymouth Belvedere with 150,000 miles on its slant-six motor. Donald Ray believed that few miles on a slant six meant it was barely broken in. One small problem with the car was the lack of seats. There were no seats in the front or back. Red had used them to sit on in his brand-new shop out behind the house. His buddies came by each morning to discuss the woes of the world and spit "tabaky juice" on Red's woodburning stove. There would be a loud hiss, a puff of steam, and nothing but a white-line stain remaining where it hit the stove. The car seats made comfy "sittin" for his buddies.

The motor was good, so was the transmission, and the car was the most beautiful bright red we had ever seen. Just no seats! Did I mention it was bright red?

Red had bolted down two bright-orange milk crates for the front seats. An old feather-tick pillow sat atop the crates for comfort. The car still had seat belts, and they worked just fine with the milk crates. We bought the car for $200. That was a lot of money in those days. Did I mention it was bright red?

Neither of us was old enough for a driver's license. Since I was the oldest and the biggest, it was decided I should drive the car until we could get it licensed. That way, we wouldn't draw as much attention to ourselves.

We drove all the back roads we could until we got home. As was the custom, we had dubbed the car "Old Red" after the previous owner. We always named everything and usually the name started out with "Old" like Old Blue, Old Roscoe, etc. We had no incidents with the law and got home just as we ran out of gas and the driver's front tire went flat.

After we got home, we did a complete inspection of the car. We decided it was good that there was no back seat. We could cut a piece of plywood to fit atop the differential hump, creating a flat surface for a bed. We could camp in our car. This was just too cool, man. We had enough money left over to buy an 8-track player, some cheap speakers, and gas for our trip. Now all we had to do was convince Granny and Gramps and Ma and Pa to let us go.

The more we planned and schemed, the more we realized there was no way in this world or any other that our parents would let us drive to New York. Not to mention the small detail of no license, it was a long way to New York and a concert for hippies wouldn't be a place we should be. There was only one way this was going to work. We agreed to tell them we were going John Wayne'n for a couple of weeks. They would never know we went to New York instead. I hope they never read this book. We never did tell them about the craziest adventure we ever had.

Donald Ray had calculated how much money we would need for gas both ways. We made out lists for food and clothes. We put together a first aid kit and, of course, bought some great 8-track tapes. We had Jimi Hendrix, Joan Baez, Joe Cocker, and Chuck Berry. We were set.

Oh, yeah. We also had incense and identical headbands. They were made of braided leather with a ceramic centerpiece that sat in the middle of the forehead. The emblem looked a lot like one of them there mary-wany plant leaves. Aside from the fact that wearing twin headbands was kind of duffy, we thought we looked cool. Hey, we were country boys, not hippies. What did we know? Right?

The night before our adventure began, Donald Ray slept over at my house. We got up and tried to act nonchalant. We talked about John Wayne'n and fishing just like we were really going. We might have made a bit too much of it because Granny was acting a little suspicious. Granny had this sixth sense about boys. She always knew when they were up to no good.

"How long you boys gonna be gone?"

"Two weeks, maybe less," I replied.

"You gonna miss church?" Granny asked insistently, looking directly into my eyes.

"Only once. We probably will get hungry for some of your cookin' before that and come home early."

I was stuffing my mouth with fried eggs and bacon, thinking about my next meals on the road and doing my best to avoid Granny's eyes. We finally finished eating and got all our gear stashed in the back of the car. We had a full tank of gas, enough grub to last a month, hopefully enough gas to get us there and back and, of course, our tickets to get into the concert. Donald Ray and I had no clue about what we were in for.

As I turned the car around to head out, Granny called out from the porch, "Keep that car off the blacktop. It ain't licensed or insured. You boys'll end up in the pokey if the sheriff catches you drivin' without a license."

Yep, she was wise to us. If she only knew.

The first leg of the trip went pretty smoothly. We camped in our car at roadside rest areas and drove long shifts. Somewhere just outside of Akron, Ohio, we realized we were not going to have enough money to make the trip and get back home. Gas was higher out on the road. We paid as much as forty-nine cents a gallon in a couple of places. That was nearly twice as much as we paid back home.

We were taking a break in a rest area when a Chevy van pulled in beside us. Someone had painted on the side of the van a sign that said, "Woodstock or bust." I started up a conversation with a guy who crawled out of the side sliding door.

"So you guys are headed to Woodstock?"

"Yeah, man, it's the most far-out thing on this planet, man. We haven't found any tickets yet, but we will when we get there. Peace, brother. Love is all you need."

"That's cool, man," I said as I thought about our dilemma. "Donald Ray."

"What?" Donald muttered as he awakened from a deep thought.

"These guys are looking for tickets to the same concert we're going to. Maybe we should just go ahead and sell ours so we can have enough gas money to get home." Donald Ray sat up like a shot.

"That's a great idea. I was just pondering what would happen if I had to call Pa to wire us money."

Donald Ray told me to get all I could for the tickets. I casually sauntered up to the driver of the van.

"You guys interested in a couple of tickets to the Woodstock concert?"

"Yeah, man, it's a total bummer. We couldn't find a ticket anywhere back in Denver. You got some?"

"I just happen to have two tickets. What are they worth to you?"

"Far out, man! How much?"

"I need forty-five dollars each," I replied.

"Would you take an OZ of some killer Acapulco Gold for one of them?"

"No way, man. I need the cash."

"No problem, man. You got a deal."

We made the exchange and parted company. We left the rest area in a hurry in case those guys decided to change their minds.

"You got how much?" Donald Ray asked.

"I got ninety for the pair." I wasn't sure if he was happy surprised or mad surprised.

"That means we now have enough money to go on up to Woodstock and back with change left over," Donald said, slapping my back.

"Maybe we can hear the concert from outside."

We still had no idea what we were about to be a part of.

The rest of the trip was pretty uneventful except for the rain. It started raining the moment we hit the New York state line and didn't stop. We got lost a few times trying to get there. The location of the concert was not actually in Woodstock. When we finally made it, we were not prepared for what we saw.

Both of us had been to major events before. We had both been to the state fair in Sedalia and figured nothing could be bigger than that. Man, were we wrong. There was a sea of muddy humanity wandering around, lying in the rain, and sitting on top of cars. Everywhere you looked, there were people.

The fence around the farmer's property where the concert was being held was lying flat on the ground where we parked. We were parked about a quarter mile from the entrance.

Both of us were comfortable about being in the country. What we weren't comfortable with was so many people. We saw things I can't go into except to say I know why they called us the generation of free love. We spent two days and nights fighting mud, rain, and some very unsanitary conditions. The organizers of the concert obviously had no idea how many Port-A-Johns they would need for this gathering. They were filled to overflowing on the first day. Others were brought in, but the numbers were insignificant for the crowd.

The concert was great. We saw groups we had heard of and many we had not. I will never forget Joe Cocker and Crosby, Stills, Nash, and Young. My favorite was Country Joe and The Fish. Remember them? "One, two, three four, what are we fighting for? Don't ask me, I don't give a damn, next stop is Viet Nam."

That was an experience neither of us will ever forget. If you ever run into either Donald Ray or me, ask us about bathing in the farmer's pond. Better yet, don't!

The last day of the concert was groovy. The rain had stopped, and celebrations were going on everywhere in typical sixties style. We loaded up the next morning with no sleep and headed home. We reached the most beautiful sight I had ever seen, the Missouri state line, in two days. My city ways had faded by this time in my life, and I was as "Missouri Country" as my running mate. We had decided that, if we got back in time, we would drive down to our usual John Wayne'n site and rest up for a couple days. The next two days were spent reflecting on a trip that had swept one country boy and one not-so-country boy into the pages of history. The stories we could tell about that experience cold fill another book. Far out, man!

CHAPTER 19

Gasconade Redhorse

Sydney Ralston, his wife, Kathleen, and a fat, ornery cat lived just across the road from us in a small Forest Service house. Sydney was the forester for the national forest in the area where our farm was. A fire tower (pronounced "far tar" in my neck of the woods), standing tall, cast a shadow over his house. The tiny, one-bedroom house had a hand pump in the kitchen that drew water from a cistern. An outhouse in the backyard met their personal needs. Sydney used a detached garage as a shop for melting down wheel weights to make fishing jigs. There was one thing Sydney loved more than life itself—fishing.

Sydney was an interesting fellow. He was short in stature standing at five feet seven inches. When it came to knowledge of nature and the outdoors, he stood a head above all others. He could look at a stand of timber and estimate the board feet of lumber in that stand with the use of nothing but a notched stick he kept under the seat of his Forest Service green, crew-cab Dodge pickup.

Sydney really liked fishing for Redhorse carp in the Osage Fork of the Gasconade River. It was quite an ordeal to fish for Redhorse with Sydney. Before any fishing took place, the bait had to be secured. I guess Redhorse carp were picky eaters. Worms were not acceptable. According to Sydney, they would only bite a piece of freshwater mussel. Being a fly-fisherman, I never used bait, but I enjoyed helping Sydney catch his.

We would beach the boat at the tail of a shoal. The water needed to be fairly fast, clear, and about a foot deep. We would walk upstream so we could peer through clear, undisturbed water into the gravel on the stream bottom. It was pretty tricky stuff. The mussels were not easy to find. They were buried in the gravel with just the top edge of their shells exposed. It is just like hunting morel mushrooms in the spring. Once you spotted one, it made it easier to find more. You developed an eye for it.

After finding a sufficient number for Sydney to fish with, we began a day of fishing. Usually, I would wade fish and let Sydney sit in the boat anchored in a deep, fast-moving run where the redhorse liked to hang out. I was almost always looking for smallmouth bass since they liked the same kind of water.

One warm summer morning we were floating downstream to a likely mussel bed when the current pulled us under a low-hanging willow. I'm still not sure about the next few seconds, but in that time frame, a very large and aggressive cottonmouth snake dropped from the willow tree into our boat. I remember a flash of movement from the corner of my eye. My eyes were glued to the very unhappy and venomous snake coiled only two or three feet from my bare toes. That flash of movement ended in a boat-shuddering *thunk!* Where the snake's head had been weaving back and forth menacingly a shovel blade stood erect. The snake's head was on one side of the shovel blade, and its body laid writhing on the other side.

Sydney had grabbed what my grandfather always called a sharp-shooter shovel. It had a blade that was long and narrow with a short handle. It was ideal for digging a narrow trench, or as Sydney determined, it was great for digging worms. When Sydney came down just behind the snake's head, he must have forgotten we were in an aluminum boat. The shovel had gone clean through the bottom of the craft.

When Sydney tried to pull the shovel out of the hole, water started to pour in. He quickly pushed the shovel back into place and stuffed a rag in around it. I didn't say a word. When I tried to toss the snake out of the boat, he quickly stopped me. Sydney always talked really fast for an Ozarkian.

"Leave it be. If somebody wants to know why we has a shovel stuck through the boat, I wanna show 'em," he said hastily.

I nodded in agreement and with some degree of understanding.

We fished the rest of that morning with some success. We had to bail water from a slight leak every thirty minutes or so. I caught and landed a nice twenty-inch smally (smallmouth bass) that day, so a little baling was no trouble at all. We didn't have to answer any embarrassing questions about that shovel acting as a main mast all day, and that made the trip a total success. Neither Sydney nor I ever mentioned that little incident again.

CHAPTER 20

Tit in a Ringer

Almost every language on earth has its phrases rooted deeply in the history of the people it belongs to. Generations come and go. The phrases sometimes lose their identity. There is no memory of how that particular phrase found its way into the lives of the people who use it. Some of the phrases can really spark the imagination, with many possible scenarios describing their origins. Others, on the other hand, leave nothing to the imagination. They mean just exactly what they say, and they originated from an obvious history.

When my granny decided to take a chance and step into the modern world of technology, she wouldn't completely give up on the old ways. When she bought her first automatic washer and dryer, she held on to her old wringer washer. Man, I hated that thing. I was the one who had to carry the heated water in five-gallon buckets for the wash water and the rinse water. That was the most boring and mundane job you could imagine for a kid my age. I wanted to be out in the woods or fishing.

One fine spring day Granny announced as she did each spring, "Today is washday."

This did not refer to putting a load or two in the automatic washer. This was the announcement I dreaded. I had to drag the old ringer washer out of the garage, start a big fire (that part was okay), and heat water in two five-gallon buckets. This process would absolutely kill a Saturday.

Granny did not believe that her automatic washer could manage to wash her winter quilts. There was only one way to get them clean to be packed away until next fall. They had to be ringer washed and line dried. That's all there was to that.

"Bring me another bucket of hot water!"

That is what I lived for on washing day.

"Why couldn't she just use that darned washer in the house? Why did she have to use this antique piece of junk?" I mumbled under my breath as I carried another bucket of hot water from the fire to the washer.

When I got there, Granny was struggling with a good-sized quilt. She got one end of it in the ringer and was running it through. The quilt was big, water soaked, and heavy.

My Granny stood four feet, eight inches tall. She was almost as wide as she was tall. She was rather busty, as was the case with many women of her size and weight. Now, don't get me wrong. My granny might have been a bit overweight and pretty darned short, but she could turn into Hulk Hogan if you riled her. She had a pretty-mean right hook too. I knew an old boy who could testify to that. But that's another story.

Anyway, back to washing day. When I reached the washer and poured in the water, Granny told me to grab on to the end of the quilt coming through and pull. I grabbed the end of the quilt flattened out by the ringer and gave a pull. Surprisingly, it didn't budge. I grabbed it with both hands, planted my feet firmly, and gave it a mighty jerk. The quilt succumbed to my effort like butter does to a hot knife.

It came through so quickly Granny lost her balance and fell forward. She had always worried about getting a hand or arm caught in the wringer, and in fact, the idea scared her to death. As she fell forward, she jerked both her arms back in defense.

There was one big problem with that particular defensive move. Her right breast fell against the wringer, and it grabbed her so fast she didn't have time to avoid it. With a scream that a Florida panther would respect, she slammed down on the lever that released the two rollers and pulled back so hard she landed flat on her bottom. I stood in shock as I witnessed an instant replay of the actual event that must have started that phrase.

"Granny? Is that what they mean by getting your tit in a wringer?"

I had heard her use that phrase more than once. She looked up at me and laughed louder and longer than I ever remember her doing in her ninety-one years of life. God bless you, Granny. I miss you. You made my life richer with your great sense of humor. Now the angels are laughing with you.

CHAPTER 21

Granny's Backside Bottle Rocket

Our community was small and close. We always celebrated the Fourth of July together down on the Roubidoux. Directly below the old Flesher place the county gravel road crossed the creek. The crossing was a low-water bridge with no railings and a set of parallel metal plates spanning the river on a wooden structure. The metal plates were spaced so the tires of a vehicle were on the metal. The bridge was a great spot to set off fireworks because the metal plates protected the bridge from the hot flames.

Immediately on the far side of the creek was a small clearing nestled against a bluff in the woods. The clearing wasn't actually a clearing. The trees were left standing, but the brush was cleared and mowed. A picnic table and a fire pit declared the spot a community picnic area. A steep, rocky path rose ten feet above the level of the road and ended at the picnic area. This gave a good vantage point for the adults sitting in lawn chairs to keep the kids in line when they got a little goofy with the dangerous explosives they were lighting on the bridge.

The last Fourth of July I celebrated at the bridge was in my sixteenth year. I was getting a little old to hang out with the young'uns and felt a little silly setting off black cats, snakes, fountains, and whirly gigs. I brought some bottle rockets and a couple of really big rockets to set off as a grand finale.

I was getting bored pretty quickly after about two dozen bottle rockets and somewhat irritated at having to keep telling the little kids to stay away from them. One bottle rocket in particular caused me a great deal of grief and embarrassment. I had just lit the fuse when a ten-year-old walked up and knocked it over. I knew that, if it went off on the bridge, every parent and grandparent there would be hollering at me to be careful around the young'uns.

I grabbed the bottle rocket and tried to place it at the forty-five-degree angle it was initially set at for launching. Just as I let go of it, the rocket fell over and launched simultaneously. The intended coordinates for the launch had been a flight up the Roubidoux with a loud report over the water. The new coordinates had the rocket flying directly into the picnic area where all the adults were sitting.

Granny did not see the rocket heading directly at her as she stood to go pour herself another glass of lemonade. I witnessed in slow motion what happened next. The rocket hit Granny dead square in the middle of her back and exploded. She let out a startled "Whoop!" Her arms flew up, and she lost her balance, falling backward.

Granny rolled down the steep embankment toward the cold water below with a pitcher of lemonade in one hand and a glass in the other. She hit a small knoll and went airborne for about two feet, landing in four feet of water. Gramps saw Granny rolling and bouncing toward the river and jumped to his feet. When she hit the water and came up sputtering and threatening whatever young'un that was responsible for trying to kill her, Gramps began to laugh. Man, was I glad he did. Granny got so mad at Gramps for laughing at her she forgot to launch an investigation to discover the culprit who shot her with a bottle rocket.

It took all the men there to haul Granny out of the river and up the steep bank. Slipping and sliding, they all fell at least once before they dragged her to the top of the bank wet, muddy, and steaming mad. July or not, Granny started to chill in her wet clothes. The party was over.

We got Granny home and into some dry clothes. She was still cussing Gramps, who would erupt into eye-watering laughter spontaneously. Granny never did ask who shot her.

Every time she told that story, my poor old Gramps was the scoundrel who ruined Granny's Fourth of July picnic. I found out years later that Gramps had watched as I tried to right the rocket that was knocked over. He knew that I had not intended for the accident to happen. He never did tell Granny any differently. Gramps had shoulders as broad as a barn. He watched out for me and would quietly stand up for me anytime he thought it was right. Every boy needs a hero. Gramps was, is, and always will be my hero.

CHAPTER 22

Cotton Mouth

Summer vacation is the best. No cows to feed, no ice to cut, and shorts and tennis shoes are all that is needed to be fully dressed. I woke to the traditional smell of frying bacon and coffee brewing in the kitchen. I grabbed some clean underwear and slipped on my cut-off shorts and my worn-out "tenny floppers," as I liked to call them. Mine looked like they had experienced a blowout at ninety miles an hour. The sides of the shoes showed my little toe, but the soles still had some wear left in 'em, so they were perfect for what I used 'em for. They were my official Roubidoux Creek wading shoes.

"Young'un, why do you keep wearing those nasty ol' worn-out tennis shoes?" Granny scowled as I entered the kitchen.

"I'm headed to the creek to catch supper," I proclaimed, feeling like the great hunter going after a woolly mammoth for the tribe's winter meat.

"After you eat some breakfast," she insisted.

"Are you kidding, Granny? I wouldn't miss a breakfast you cooked."

"I'll fix you a sack lunch to take along. Be home by two o'clock."

I nodded acknowledgement with a mouth full of biscuit slathered with molasses and butter.

Everything I needed was waiting for me on the back porch, ready to go. My fly rod, a double-sided fly box loaded with hand-made poppers and some assorted bass and bluegill flies, a nylon-rope stringer, and an old willow Creel for my lunch. I stuffed an egg-and-bacon sandwich, a cold biscuit with butter and molasses, a pint mason jar filled with sweet tea, and an orange into the willow Creel. Along with the lunch was a pint-milk carton filled with water and frozen solid. As the water melted in the paper milk carton, the willow Creel would allow the water to drip out without soaking the food. It wasn't the most efficient way to keep food from spoiling, but it was cheap. I never got sick from food kept cool in this manner. A number of years later we were able to go high tech when plastic milk jugs hit the markets.

The sun was just breaking over the treetops as I walked along the gravel road toward the creek. I had walked that road so many times I knew every rock, tree, and bush by first name. I knew where to stop and move stealthily to see the deer feeding in a small field. There was a particular fox squirrel that loved to announce my presence to the rest of his wildlife neighbors. I was always trying to sneak past it. I never could outfox that foxy squirrel.

I stood at the top of the hill, looking down on the Roubidoux Creek valley below. A midsummer haze shrouded the valley below in a thin veil. The humidity had settled onto the grass during the night, giving everything a damp refreshed look, even though it hadn't rained for at least two weeks. Rocks tumbled and rolled from my steps as I walked down the steep hillside to the valley below.

A small stone flipped up into my shoe through the hole in the side and was really beginning to irritate my little toe. I stopped half-way down the hill to dislodge the stone from the inside bend of my toe. I sat down on a large rock the road grader had pushed up to the side of the ditch, running parallel to the road. A five-lined skink with an electric-blue tail scurried out from under the rock as I sat, digging the stone out from the side of my shoe. I was finally forced to take my shoe off to rid my poor toe of its irritant.

After pulling the shoe back on, I looked out over the fescue field below me, wondering if the Fleshers were going to need my help again this year putting up hay. The grass was nearly ready for cutting. The hay in that river bottom field always produced the heaviest bales of hay I ever had to buck.

I always preferred bucking as opposed to stacking. When you walked alongside the wagon tossing the bales up to the stacker, you would get the occasional breeze, giving some relief from the sweltering summer heat. The stacker, on the other hand, was surrounded by a wall of hot hay bales acting as heat radiators. It's hard but honest work.

One of these days, there won't be hay crews like we worked with. I had heard about some hay bales that weighed over 1,200 pounds and were hauled out of the field by tractors with long spikes on the front end. I couldn't imagine that they would go over very well. How in the world would a herd of cattle be able to eat from one bale of hay? There would be too much waste, and some of the cows wouldn't ever get to eat. Little did I know that the big balers would, in fact, replace the hay crews of my youth.

It wasn't because the farmers and ranchers didn't like the hay crews; it was because nobody wanted to work that hard, and the farmers and ranchers couldn't hire good crews. This forced a labor-market change. Farmers had to have a way to put up their hay and feed it without the help of hired crews.

What a shame. The values I learned from that kind of hard work are what made me the person I am today. I'm not afraid of hard work or getting my hands dirty. There was also camaraderie with the crew you worked with during the haying season. You might not see the same guys through the rest of the year, but when haying season rolled around, the crew would all come together again to work as a team and get the job done. Many times we would work late into the night if a threat of rain loomed on the horizon. We had to get the man's hay in before it got wet. That was the way it was, and that was all there was to it.

I remember the lunches during the hay season fondly. The wife of whoever's farm you were on at the time would prepare lunch for the entire crew. If you have never experienced an old-fashioned, Ozark-style hay-crew lunch, you are missing the experience of a lifetime. Imagine, if you will, a table—actually, three eight-foot-long tables—placed end to end. We are talking about twenty-four feet of food stretched out before you. There is meat, of course. Feast your eyes on large platters filled with mounds of fried chicken, roast pork, roast beef, and sausages. Notice I did not say "Or." I said, "And."

Past the meat you come to the beans. There are home-canned green beans with chunks of bacon and sliced onions steaming in a huge bowl. Next to the green beans are baked beans sweet and tangy, and we can't forget the navy beans thick and cooked to perfection with green onions by the pound ready to be consumed with the beans. Past the beans are platters of corn on the cob, with real butter melting down the sides, green salad, macaroni salad, tuna salad, potato salad, fresh-baked bread straight from the oven with loads of home-canned jams and jellies, honey and molasses.

My favorite was the desserts. Pecan pie, cherry cobbler, peach cobbler, and donuts covered the far end of the table. The donuts were always the first to go. The cook would use canned biscuits, roll them out, and cut a hole in the center. The donuts were then deep fried and rolled in sugar while they were still hot. My mouth is watering as I write this.

I think I would be willing to work in the hayfields again just for one of those lunches. We were always allowed an hour nap after lunch to sleep it off before we started work for the afternoon. The entire crew would be stretched out under the shade of a tree or under the hay wagon, snoring within minutes. The farmer's wife would always ring the dinner bell when she finished cleaning up from lunch. That was our signal to shake off the sleep and get back to work.

I reached the low-water bridge that crossed the Roubidoux and stepped onto the soft sand along the edge of the road. I already had a popper tied on and was ready to start catching some fish. The water felt freezing cold for the first thirty seconds but quickly became very comfortable as I got used to the temperature change.

I waded into a run that was about four feet deep and tortured myself by slowly lowering into the water until it reached my crotch. Finally, I just plopped down into a seated position and went completely under to get the agony over. Man, it felt great! I stood up, dripping wet and feeling very refreshed. Time to fish.

There are few things in life that compare to the enjoyment of wet wading on a warm summer morning and catching one nice-sized sunfish after another. The morning sun shone against the left bank as I waded downstream. Bright shafts of light penetrated the gin-clear water next to the banks, exposing the dark silhouettes of the pan-sized fish I hunted.

I cast a small yellow popping bug and watched it drop lightly onto the surface directly above a bright circle of gravel. Suspended just above the gravel was a large male bluegill protecting a nest. Male bluegill, unlike many fish, were the chosen protectors of the nest and even stayed with the young fry until they were old enough to go out on their own. The immediate response of any male bluegill on the nest was to protect it from any threat. When the popper dropped onto the surface of the water directly above him, he viciously grabbed it in his mouth to take it away from the nest. I watched as he rose to the fly and sucked it into his mouth. I set the hook immediately, and the fight was on.

While fighting this feisty creature, I noticed a small bass move into the nest, feeding on the young bluegill. I guided the bluegill back to the nest to scare off the bass. It worked for a second or two, but just as soon as the bluegill fought its way off the nest, the bass was back managing the bluegill population.

I brought the large male to hand and slipped one end of the rope stringer behind its gill plate and out through the mouth. This does not injure the fish, so they stayed alive long enough to stay fresh until I was ready to clean them for supper. In a short time, I had six nice bluegills on my stringer. I thought that eight would be my stopping number. That way, Gramps and I would have three to eat and Granny two. That was all she would ever eat at one time. Two more to go.

I felt the captive "gills" tugging on the stringer tied to my belt loop and felt pretty good about my fishing trip. I had released nearly twice as many smaller fish and had only kept the larger ones. They would make nice fillets.

The tugging on my belt loop became more insistent, and then I felt something brush against my leg. It didn't feel like a fish. I peered down through the water at my stringer. A very large and extremely venomous cottonmouth snake had one of my bluegills in its mouth and was trying, with much difficulty, to swallow it. I wasn't going to quarrel with that bad boy, so I very carefully untied the stringer from my belt loop and gently guided the stringer out and away from my trembling legs.

When I had my arm extended as far from my body as possible, I let the stringer slip from my fingers. The slow low-water flow of the current pulled the stringer of fish sluggishly away finally, settling it into a hole of water just deep enough to take on a slightly bluish tint. I could see the bright underside of a fish struggling to free itself from the jaws of the cottonmouth.

The snake tried to swim out of the deep water with its prize, but was held down by the weight of the full stringer. I stood frozen in fear and fascination as I watched it try to claim its trophy. Only the tail of the snake could break the surface of the water as it writhed its way to the surface. The need for life-giving oxygen finally decided the end of the show. The snake let go of the fish and swam to the surface.

It looked around and seemed to measure me up and down. There was no doubt in my mind that it was deciding whether to bite me out of frustration, or to just move on down the creek. I wanted to run and scream like a lunatic. I *couldn't.* My feet had grown deep roots and would not pull free from the stream bottom. The snake decided to carry on with whatever business it was up to before it came across my stringer of fish.

I watched it swim with its undulating side-to-side movement until I could no longer see it. I looked down at my stringer of fish. They were all still there but slowly started to move downstream. They all seemed to be of one mind and were working together to get away from the human with the fly rod. I stretched out my rod, hooked the stringer with its tip, and drew it to me. I had my fish back.

The fish the snake had tried to swallow was dead. I was afraid it had been pumped full of venom, and didn't want anything to do with it. I slid it off the stringer and threw it with all my might in the direction of the snake. Maybe it would find the fish and finish its meal and leave me alone for the rest of the day. I secretly hoped it would choke on a fish spine or something.

Now I needed three more fish to complete my objective. I decided I would fish my way back upstream in the opposite direction of the snake. By the time I reached the bridge, I had all eight fish strung and had almost stopped shivering from the "scare-the-devil-outa-you" experience with the cottonmouth.

I untied the stringer of fish and tied them to a waterside willow so they would stay wet while I ate my lunch. Lunch was even better than I had hoped. The warm morning sun shone down on my face as I laid back in the soft sand. Sleep came on so fast I didn't even realize I had gone to sleep.

A tickle on my face awoke me from a dream about snakes squirming over my face and hands. A black wood ant was scurrying across my cheek. I wiped it away quickly with a start and sat up. I had been asleep for only a few minutes. A splash from the stringer of fish reminded me where I was and what I was doing. I lifted the stringer from the water and was relieved to find that no snake was in sight. It had to be time to head home.

I trudged up the steep hill from the Roubidoux Creek bottoms, turning at the top of the hill to look once more over the valley below. Yep, I needed to give the Fleshers a call about hay season. I needed to make a few bucks. I really wanted to buy one of those metal stingers I saw at Bennett Spring the last time Gramps and I went fishing there. *A new pair of tennis shoes might not be a bad investment too*, I thought as a small stone flipped in through the hole in the side of my shoe and lodged under my small toe.

CHAPTER 23

Smells Like Cigars to Me!

What is it that makes for a good story? Is it someone who is good at telling one or is it the story itself? I would venture to say that it takes both. If you throw in a lesson or two mixed with a touch of humor and a whole lot of believability, you have the perfect scenario for a good story. This story has most of the necessary ingredients. It has some humor, a definite lesson, and a full serving of believability. The only ingredient that may be questionable is the storyteller himself.

Like most boys who have access to a lot of trees, I had to have a tree fort. I searched the eighty-acre woods on our farm with a fine-tooth comb, looking for just the right tree. I found it at the edge of the woods directly above the gate that led to the fishing pond. I had passed by that tree hundreds of times and never really looked at it with the critical eye of an architect in the mood to build a tree-top mansion.

The tree stood nearly eighty feet tall. It was a white oak and would hold many of its brown leaves nearly all winter. The dead leaves would drop toward earth when the newly swollen buds on the twig ends began to open. Unlike the other species of oak inhabiting my woods that lost their leaves after the first good wind in November, this one would offer some privacy throughout the bare, cold openness of winter.

Winter was months away when I spied this remarkable tree. I rushed back to the house and started to pilfer the old lumber pile. Gramps didn't like to throw things away. Any scrap wood was thrown onto the lumber pile. There was wood in that pile that was older than the Bill of Rights. I found a couple pieces of treated 3/4-inch plywood and a bunch of two-by-four pieces.

I loaded my treasures into the wagon hitched to the back of our old 1948 Ford model 8N tractor, and drove over to Gramps's side of the garage. There I borrowed his good hammer, a brown paper sack full of nails, and a huge mud-dauber nest. Why would that stupid mud dauber build a nest inside a paper sack full of nails? Curious creatures.

I should probably explain what I mean by Gramps's side of the garage. When my grandparents bought the house from the company my grandfather worked for, they had it moved to the land they had purchased about a quarter mile down the road. The house came complete with an unattached two-car garage. They had it set in the field back behind the house. You could go through a walk-in door from the backyard, or you could enter from the pasture side through the large, overhead-style garage doors.

Both sides of the garage had their own walk-in door and garage door. Gramps had built a wall dividing the garage into his side and Granny's side. Granny's side was mostly used for storing her canning supplies, old stovepipe sections, and various and diverse good stuff.

Gramps had his side fixed up as a shop. He had a bench grinder, a vise, and boxes of really neat stuff like tools, nuts and bolts of every size imaginable, an acetylene welder, and cans of paint, varnish and non-recognizable liquids that probably belonged in a hazardous-waste site.

Granny's side of the garage was open to anyone interested in going into it. Gramps's side, on the other hand, was a sacred temple, and only the invited and initiated were allowed in. I had been initiated with long lectures about putting tools back where you found them, blah, blah, blah. So I could come and go as I saw the need. I was even allowed to know where the key to the monster padlock that secured the heavy overhead garage door was covertly hidden. If there was also a secret handshake, I hadn't been privy to that information at my early age.

I drove the tractor, pulling the trailer loaded with building materials to the edge of the woods directly under my selected tree. The first order of business was to nail some short two-by-fours for steps up to a large branch about twenty feet above the ground. There were actually two branches that had grown straight out from the tree trunk, forming a "V" where they joined the trunk. I laid a four-foot by four-foot piece of treated 3/4-inch plywood across the two branches and nailed them down. I now had a solid platform for my tree house. After putting up a couple of short walls and a roof high enough so that I could stand in my tree fort, I was ready to call it a day.

I sat in my tree fort for a few minutes, imagining all the great times I would have in it. Out of the blue, a voice called up to me from below.

"You up there?"

I stuck my head out one of the openings above the wall and saw my cousin, Tiger. That wasn't his real name, but that's what we called him. He was about three years younger than me, not very big, and a fistful of trouble. That boy couldn't walk through a room without doing something that would get him and anyone close to him in deep trouble. But I liked him, and the few times he and his family came out from town to the farm we had a blast.

"Can I come up?"

"You know the secret password?"

"Sure do."

"Well, what is it?" I said, doubting very much that he knew since I had not decided on one yet.

"Cigar," he responded (pronounced see-gar with a long, drawn-out *E*). I looked at him inquisitively. He reached into his back pocket and pulled out two cigars wrapped in gold-colored cellophane. "Canadian Sweets," he proudly proclaimed as I waved him up.

Tiger pulled out a book of matches and handed me a cigar. I had never smoked before and wasn't sure about the whole thing. I thought kids who smoked went blind or something.

"You smoked these before?" I asked.

"Yep. Bunches of times."

Actually, he had never smoked one, and I could tell he was lying through his teeth. He wouldn't admit that he hadn't, even if his life depended on it.

"Do you inhale?"

"Of course, I do," he said, looking sheepishly like Pinocchio right before his nose started to grow.

"Light yours first," I said, holding the cigar between my fingers and not knowing which end to light.

Tiger struck a match like a pro. He tentatively held the flame to the end of the cigar and drew in on it to light it. His cheeks puffed out like two small balloons as he tried to stifle a cough. When he couldn't hold it back, he coughed so hard he blew out the match.

After a short coughing spell, he puffed on his cigar and blew the smoke out of his mouth.

"Mm, good smoke," he said with an air of maturity that neither of us possessed.

He leaned back against the trunk of the tree and drew in another puff of smoke. He held it in his mouth, trying to look as if he inhaled it, and blew it out, pretending to blow a smoke ring.

"Light up, man," he insisted.

I took the book of matches he handed me and tried lighting my cigar. I sucked the flame into the dry tobacco and inhaled. Smoke filled my lungs, and I started to cough vehemently. I coughed and coughed. My stomach began to feel nauseated, either from the coughing or from the tobacco. I'm not sure which, but in either case, I leaned out of the tree fort just in time to puke all over the tractor seat directly below me.

"You okay, man?"

I shook my head between fits of coughing, gagging, and dry heaving.

"You look green, man. Did you inhale that smoke?"

My eyes were watering, and my lungs felt like they were filled with red-hot coals. I was extremely sick to my stomach. All I wanted to do was lay down and die.

I nodded my head to his question. He looked at me with sympathetic eyes and shook his head.

"Man, you shouldn't inhale on your first cigar. You could go blind or something."

I was afraid I was going to because everything was blurry through my watering eyes.

I was secretly hoping that a stray bullet from a hunter's gun would find its way through the woods to my tree fort and strike me dead. I felt so bad. The one thing I didn't want to happen did.

"You boys need to come in for supper!" Granny was calling from the backyard.

I answered her so she wouldn't come out to the tree fort. I had stopped coughing, but was still very nauseated.

"Okay, Granny. We'll be right there."

It took all the strength I had not to gag between my words. I threw that cigar just as far as I could and started down the steps to the ground.

"I'm not throwing my cigar away," Tiger said as he was putting the nasty thing out on the floor of my new tree fort.

He then shoved it into his jeans pocket. I ran down to the pond and got a bucket of water to wash the puke off the tractor seat, and we started toward the house. When I walked into the kitchen, the smell of food made me gag involuntarily.

Granny looked at me and asked, "You okay, young'un? You look pretty puny."

"I don't feel very good, Granny. I think I must be coming down with something."

About that time, Tiger walked into the kitchen, all smiles and innocence. As he walked by Granny, she grabbed his shoulder and looked him right in the eyes.

"Don't even try to lie to me, boy. I smell a nasty old cigar on you. Empty your pockets."

He pulled a crumbled cigar out of his pocket and just stared at the floor.

Granny looked at me and shook her head.

"You're lucky all you got was sick. You could have went blind, smoking them nasty things. Go wash up for supper."

CHAPTER 24

The Rope

The dog days of summer are the hottest part of the year. Steamy, sweltering, wilting, and "too darned hot" are all descriptions of a late summer in Missouri. Early afternoon temperatures in the upper nineties with humidity at 89 percent drew Donald Ray and me toward a deep-blue, spring-fed hole of water on the Roubidoux for cooling off. A giant sycamore tree leaned out over the stream, creating the perfect trajectory to swing out over the water. The tree seemed to beg for a rope and a couple of daring boys to swing from it.

Since we always carried emergency supplies in the trunk of Old Red like tools, a spare tire, two boxes of wooden matches that would strike anywhere, a canteen for water, a sleeping bag, a tarp, an iron skillet, and about one hundred feet of good rope, we were more than happy to accommodate that old sycamore tree.

Donald shimmied up the tree with the rope coiled over his shoulder and tied it to the highest section of the tree he could reach. I stood on the bank, watching as he climbed down, using the rope to make his way to a good-sized limb that stood out at a right angle to the tree trunk about twenty-five feet above the water.

Donald balanced his ninety-pound, tough-as-nails, skinny self on the limb. Holding onto the rope tightly, he leaped off into space.

It was poetry in motion. He dropped from the limb, holding tightly to the rope. He had calculated the exact location on the rope for a good swinging arch. He glided through the air like a pendulum, arching up and out over the deepest part of the pool. At just the right moment he let go of the rope and flew through the air, rising higher and higher until gravity tugged him toward the cold, inviting waters of the Roubidoux. A perfectly executed cannonball produced a splash that anyone would be proud of.

It was my turn. I climbed the side of the sycamore with the skill of a one-armed monkey with a bad itch. I positioned myself to drop from the tree, holding the rope at the exact spot I had determined I should because of my height. I stood nearly a foot above my best friend and outweighed him by eighty-five pounds, so his spot didn't work for me.

I gripped the rope tightly and leaped off into space. Down I went, holding the rope closely to my chest. I was going to swing out over that stream and fly like an eagle.

The rope straightened in my hands, and my body felt the G force as the rope and I hit the bottom of the arch. This was where the momentum of the swing would initiate my flight over the Roubidoux. I was ready.

At that precise moment I realized I was in trouble. There was no way I would be able to hold my own weight compounded with the high-speed downward momentum of my descent. The rope burned through my fingers, and it felt as if tiny hooks were ripping the flesh from my hands. I squeezed the rope tighter, pressing it against my chest and belly, unwilling to fail. I felt the rope burning a groove in my chest and belly as the weight of my body exceeded the ability of my hands and arms to hold tightly to the rope.

I hit the muddy edge of the stream feet first, driving deep into the soft ooze. My hands, belly, and chest felt as if they were smoking. I attempted to dive headfirst toward the cool water to quench the burning. My feet didn't move. I was stuck knee-deep in soft mud, with only an inch of muddy water to cool my burning hands. I had landed inches from the edge of the stream, far short of the cooling waters I was attempting to reach.

Donald just stood there with an amused look on his face. It's a good thing when something this humbling happens to you that it happens in front of your best friend and not someone else. I knew he would never forget what he saw that day, nor would it be retold to anyone except occasionally to me when he felt I needed to be humbled.

Donald was always thinking of ways to do things more efficiently. That was a trait that most people born with a lazy gene shared in common.

He tried tying a large knot in the rope for me to hold onto. It didn't work. I went down like a paratrooper with a concrete parachute.

He then tried tying another knot in the rope to stand on with my bare feet. That didn't work either. I would be plagued with extra-high arches for the rest of my life from that attempt. Finally, he took a good-sized dead tree limb that still felt solid enough to support me and tied it to the rope so I could sit on it and swing out. That worked, except for one small problem. It's hard to let go when you're sitting on the stick. The first time I tried it, I swung all the way back to the tree and nearly knocked myself out when I crashed into it.

I finally mastered the technique of sliding off the stick, not smacking myself in the mouth with it, and dropping safely to the water. What a glorious day it was. With Donald's propensity for mechanics and some major bruising, I beat the rope.

The sky presented a sunset of red, orange, and violet when we decided to head for home.

"Looks like another clear sky tomorrow," Donald said as we jumped in Old Red and started up the '62 Plymouth Belvedere. Donald was a firm believer in the old sayings like "Red sky at night, sailors delight."

"You probably ought to put some cow-teat salve on those rope burns when you get home," he advised.

I nodded silently, thinking an aspirin or two might be in order as well.

EPILOGUE

I wouldn't give up one minute of my life in the Ozarks. I believe fly-fishing, Granny and Gramps, and my best friend, Donald Ray, saved my life. Had I not made that journey all those years ago, I am certain I would not be here today. The passion for conservation and fisheries my grandparents instilled in me as a boy has decided my lot in life.

Donald Ray has grown up to be a cattle farmer still on the family farm. His two boys show promise of following in their father's footsteps. One of the boys looks and acts just like his dad. I look forward to the time I spend with those two boys. They take me back to the days when Donald Ray and I were the terrors of Texas County. Well, at least in our minds we were.

Most of the old-timers we knew are long gone. Donald Ray and I decided that we are now the old-timers. It is our turn to shake our heads at the foolishness of today's generation and to worry ourselves sick about where they are and what they're doing.

When I have the opportunity to go back to the community that was so special to me, it's like time has stood still. Sure, the cars are newer, and folks have cell phones, but the way of life, the wonderful sense of humor, and especially the colorful personalities have not been affected by time and progress.

My beloved Roubidoux Creek hasn't changed much. When the spring rains fill her banks, and the old pools are once again deep and blue, she looks as if she hasn't aged a day. The adventures, the lessons, and the love she shared will go with me anywhere I am.

—*Mark Van Patten*
December 2009